Bronson Howard

Young Mrs. Winthrop

A play in four acts

Bronson Howard

Young Mrs. Winthrop
A play in four acts

ISBN/EAN: 9783337105334

Printed in Europe, USA, Canada, Australia, Japan

Cover: Foto ©Andreas Hilbeck / pixelio.de

More available books at **www.hansebooks.com**

YOUNG MRS. WINTHROP.

A PLAY IN FOUR ACTS.

BY

BRONSON HOWARD.

Published in accordance with the requirements of the copyright law.

MADISON SQUARE THEATRE, NEW YORK,

1882.

CHARACTERS.

MRS. RUTH WINTHROP.

MR. DOUGLAS WINTHROP, HER SON.

CONSTANCE WINTHROP, HIS WIFE.

BUXTON SCOTT, A LAWYER.

MRS. DICK CHETWYN, A LADY OF SOCIETY.

EDITH, SISTER OF CONSTANCE.

HERBERT.

DR. MELLBANKE.

MAID.

We fell out, my wife and I,
O we fell out—I know not why—
And kiss'd again with tears.
For when we came where lies the child
We lost in other years;
There above the little grave,
O there above the little grave,
We kiss'd again with tears.

TENNYSON.

LULLABY.—"Golden Slumbers.

Composed by FRANK A. HOWSON.

Allegro moderato con espress.

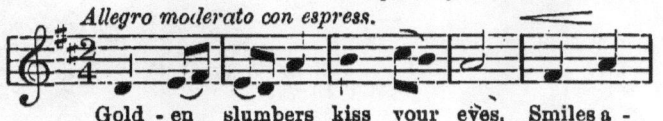

Gold - en slumbers kiss your eyes, Smiles a -

wait you when you rise ; Sleep, lit - tle

dar - ling, do not cry. And I will sing a -

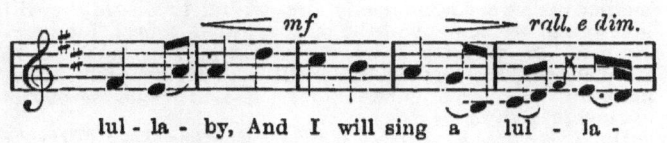

lul - la - by, And I will sing a lul - la -

by, Lul - la - by, lul - la - by.

YOUNG MRS. WINTHROP.

ACT FIRST.

SCENE.—*Interior of a private residence of a man of wealth in New York. Door* R. 1. E.; *also* R. U. E. *A mantel and fire* R., *near front. An easel, with portrait of a beautiful little girl of four years, up* C. *Small stand or table down* L. C. *A number of presents for a child's birthday, on chairs and other pieces of furniture,* C. *and* L. C. *Some of these presents must be such as are referred to in the dialogue. Evening. Lights for ordinary family life. Discovered:* MRS. RUTH WINTHROP, *sitting before fire down* R. *She has a doll, partly dressed, in her lap, and is working on its little bonnet. She is singing a lullaby, as she works, when the curtain rises.*

MRS. RUTH. There, Miss Dolly! (*Trying bonnet on the doll and holding it up*) you will have a beautiful little mother to-morrow, and I shall be your great-grandmother. Your name is to be " Ruth "—after me—how do you like it? Your little mother has a very large family already, but I am sure she will love you more than any of the rest. (*Kisses the doll.*) Lie here, my pet. (*Holding the doll to her breast.*) You must go to sleep at once, for mother Rosie will be up very early in the morning. (*Enter* DOUGLAS *up* L.) H–s–h. (*Sings as at rise of curtain, petting the doll.*)

DOUG. (*At the back of her chair, leaning over her.*) Playing with a doll, mother?

MRS. RUTH. Douglas! (*Looking up and laughing quietly.*) Yes. I had forgotten my gray hairs. I was a child again, like Rosie. We old folks grow young again in our grandchildren.

DOUG. You've never grown old, mother. You've always been living the same sweet loving life.

MRS. RUTH. (*With a quiet laugh.*) Leave any woman alone with a doll five minutes and she will be holding it to her heart without knowing it.

DOUG. (*With a sigh, up* C.) Ah! mother, I'm afraid some women outgrow it. Where is Constance?

MRS. RUTH. In her room. (*Rising.*)

DOUG.   Is she, too, at work for Rosie's birthday?

MRS. RUTH.   Well—no—not just now.   She is dressing for the reception at Mrs. Warrington's.

DOUG.   Ah! I did not know she was going.

MRS. RUTH.   You have forgotten it?   You have barely time to get ready.

DOUG.   Herbert will look after Constance.   I have another engagement; I'm going to supper at the club.   I must dress at once.   Good night, mother—if I do not see you again.

MRS. RUTH.   Good night, my son.   (*He kisses her and moves to the door up* R.)

DOUG.   (*Stopping.   Aside.*)   I asked Constance not to go to-night.   (*Exit up* R.)

MRS. RUTH.   (*Alone.   Looking after Douglas and shaking her head.*)   Douglas and Constance see less and less of each other every day.   I am *very* anxious for them.   " Business" and " the club," and the " duties of society," are changing them into mere acquaintances.   Every time I have visited them, for the last two years, I have found them more indifferent, colder to each other.   Love, even like theirs, cannot live.   It is terrible —terrible!   But I—*I* can only look on and be silent.   (*Sits* L. C.)

Enter HERBERT *up* R.

HERBERT.   (C.)   Aunt Ruth!

MRS. RUTH.   (*Seated*, L. C.)   Herbert!   What's the matter?

HER.   I've got to go to the ball to-night with Constance. Uncle Douglas isn't going.   He says he has an engagement at the club.   He always has an engagement at the club—or some-where—and he always leaves me to go out with Constance. This is the fourth time in one week.   I hate balls.   (*Crossing* R. C.)

MRS. RUTH.   You hate balls!   You were very fond of them last winter.   You went nearly every evening.

HER.   It was different then.   Where is Edith?

MRS. RUTH.   Edith?   (*Looking up significantly—then after a pause.*)   She's with Rosie.

HER.   (*After a pause.*)   Aunt Ruth, how much income ought a man to have before he can get married; not enough to make a show on, but for him and his wife to live happily to-gether?

MRS. RUTH.   That depends, my dear boy, on how much they love each other.   Two people who love each other very much can be exceedingly happy on a very moderate income.

HER.   Well—I'm sure I love her enough to be happy on nothing at all.

MRS. RUTH.   Her?

HER.   Oh!   Aunt Ruth—(*crossing to her*)—I can't talk to any one else about it; but—(*taking her hand; she looking up in his face smiling*)—everybody can talk to you.   I—I do love Edith.

MRS. RUTH.   My dear boy, I know it.

HER. My salary is only twelve hundred dollars a year; but Uncle Douglas told me to-day he will raise it to fifteen hundred after the first of March. That's because I have been working so hard—ever since I first began to—to feel that Edith might share it with me. I've saved five hundred dollars since then. I never saved a cent before. I have been wearing my old clothes, and I have my gloves cleaned—I don't care whether they smell of turpentine or not, when I go to balls, now, with Constance—and I've given up cigars. I do love Edith.

MRS. RUTH. You have chosen the very best way to make love to her; working hard and saving your money for her sake. But I will speak to you as if I were her mother, Herbert; for her own mother and her father lie side by side in the churchyard at Concord. Have you really thought what it means to marry a blind girl, like Edith?

HER. (*With enthusiasm increasing as he proceeds.*) It means, Aunt Ruth, that I shall always have to take care of her, as if she were a little child; it means that I shall be her whole world; I shall be her protector; she will depend upon me for everything; I shall have to work for her, and oh! how hard, I shall work, when she is at our home thinking of me. I love her all the more for being blind.

MRS. RUTH. You *have* thought about it, my boy. If Edith loves you, even her blindness need not keep you apart.

HER. If—she loves me. (*Sighs.*) I—I can never tell whether she does or not. She doesn't seem to know the difference between loving me and loving any of you. I might as well try to make love to little Rosie as to Edith.

MRS. RUTH. She knows as little about it as Rosie.

HER. Yes. (*With a smile.*) That's because she's blind. I love her blindness.

MRS. RUTH. No one has ever spoken to her of love or marriage. She lives in a little world of her own. You must wait for her woman's nature to assert itself in her heart.

HER. I thought, perhaps, you might help me a little.

MRS. RUTH. Help you?

HER. If you would talk to her about it, just to let her know that when *I* tell her—I love her—it isn't quite the same thing —as—as any of you loving her, you know.

MRS. RUTH. It is awkward for a young lover, isn't it, Herbert? Perhaps I can do something for you. But you are only twenty-two and Edith is only seventeen. You can both wait.

Enter CONSTANCE *up* R. *She is in full evening dress, cloak over her arm, fan, etc.* (*Crosses* C.)

CON. (*As she enters.*) Are you ready, Herbert? Not dressed yet?
HER. Eh?—Oh! (*Suddenly bolting across stage.*) It won't take me ten minutes. (*Aside.*) I hate these balls.
(*Exit up* R.)
CON. The boy is always late now. (*Taking up doll.*) You have finished Rosie's doll. What a sweet little lady she is.

(*Laughs lightly—then with a sigh.*) I could not finish the doll I was dressing for Rosie. I have had no time to do anything for my child's birthday. I was obliged to send down town at the last moment, this afternoon—and—and—buy a present for her. (*Sits* R. C.)

MRS. RUTH. (*Crossing* R. C.) And here it is. Rosie will be delighted with it.

CON. (*Shaking her head sadly.*) Rosie will love this doll better than that. Children seem to feel the difference between what is made for them with loving hands, and what is only bought with money. Rosie can look so far into one's heart with those great blue eyes of hers. I sometimes tremble when my child and I are together.

MRS. RUTH. (*Tenderly.*) When Rosie looks into your heart, Constance, I am sure she finds a great and true love there for her.

CON. (*Rises.*) It is there—yes—it is there ; but so many other things are there, too—I—I sometimes fear the child cannot always find it.

MRS. RUTH. [C.] We shall have a merry day to-morrow, Constance. Rosie will be awake long before breakfast. Edith and I have promised to be up as soon as she is, and bring her down to see the presents ;—and when you and Douglas come down—

(CONS. *suddenly strikes bell on table* R. C.)

CONS. I shall be up as early as you, mother.

MRS. RUTH. Rosie will wake before six.

Enter MAID *up* L. E.

CONS. (*To* MAID.) Have me called at five o'clock to-morrow, Jeanette.

MAID. Yes, madam. (*Exit up* L.)

MRS. RUTH. You will not be in bed before three.

CONS. If I can spare time for a fashionable ball to-night, I need not rob my child of it on her birthday. I, too, shall be with Rosie all day, to-morrow.

MRS. RUTH. Oh ! we shall have a happy day, all of us. But I fear Edith may have some difficulty in getting Rosie to sleep, the child has so many plans in her head for to-morrow. I will go to them. I hope you will have a pleasant time this evening, Constance. Good night. (*Crossing* R.)

CONS. (*Kissing her.*) Good night, mother, dear. (*Exit* MRS. RUTH R. 1 E. Shall I go to Mrs. Warrington's to-night? Douglas was very much in earnest when he asked me not to go. But he is going to his club. He is never at home. I *must* go. If I stay at home, I cannot help thinking. Oh ! if I had died before his neglect began ! I—(*slowly as if a more painful thought had come into her mind*),—I sometimes feel that Douglas and I— (*sees the child's picture.*) No ! Rosie ! She belongs to us both ! She will hold us together. (*Stands a moment in thought, then, smiling.*) How prettily she threw her arms about my neck and

kissed me good-night just now. Shall I go to Mrs. Warrington's ?

Enter MAID *up* L. *with a letter.*

MAID. A letter for Mr. Winthrop—by messenger. No
answer, madam.

CONS. I will give it to him. (*Taking letter. Exit* MAID.)
Shall I go to-night? (*Looking at letter in her hand. Raises
it to her face as if attracted by the odor.*) Violet! It is
not a business letter. A lady's handwriting! (*She turns the
letter.*) A dove and a serpent as a crest—H. D.—from Mrs.
Hepworth Dunbar. (*Leaves note on table* R. C., *and crosses
to* L.)

Enter DOUGLAS, *now in dress suit, up* R.

DOUG. Constance ! (*Stopping* C.)

CONS. Douglas ! (L. C.)

DOUG. You are in full dress, I see.

CONS. Madam de Battiste's latest inspiration. Do you like
it ?

DOUG. It is a very becoming costume, my dear.

CONS. You are in evening dress. You are going to accom-
pany me?

DOUG. I am engaged for a supper at the club with Dick
Chetwyn.

CONS. Jeanette just brought in a note for you—it is on the
table.

DOUG. Ah ! (*Turning to table.* CONSTANCE *watches him as
he opens and reads letter.*)

CONS. (*Turning away with her back toward him.*) Anything
important, Douglas ?

DOUG. (*After looking across at her quietly, then placing the
letter in his pocket.*) Merely a business matter. (*Turning to
presents* C. *and* L. C.) Rosie will be quite overwhelmed with
her birthday presents to-morrow.

CONS. (*Aside.*) Business !

DOUG. I ordered a little walnut bedstead—ah ! here it is.
A dressing-table and mirror, with cut-glass perfumery bottles,
and a box of cosmetics, and a tiny jewelry casket. (*Reads card.*)
"Mrs. Richard Chetywn." A very characteristic present.
(R. C.) Here is a magnificent doll, in full ball costume, with real
lace and a long train, and a coiffure. Another of our ultra-
fashionable friends sent that, I suppose. It does seem a
pity to put such ideas into the head of an innocent child.
(*Leans over and reads card.*) "From Rosie's mamma." (*He
glances at* CONSTANCE.) Forgive me, Constance, I was speaking thoughtlessly. Any expression of a mother's love is sacred
to me. Constance—I—I am very sorry to see you in that costume to-night.

CONS. You did not wish me to go to Mrs. Warrington's.

DOUG. Mrs. Warrington's house is a centre of a certain kind
of fashionable society in New York. The men are rich and

fast, and the wives vie with the men in the display of their riches. Constance, you have never cared for this extremely "fashionable" circle until within a year or two.

CONS.   I had no reason to seek it.

DOUG.   Reason?

CONS.   Some women find, in the gayeties of this society, something to compensate them for what they do not find at home.

DOUG.   (*Quickly.*) What do you mean, Constance?

Enter MAID *with a card in an envelope.*

MAID.   Madam—

(CONSTANCE *takes card.   Exit* MAID.)

CONS.   (*Reading card.*) "Mrs. Richard Chetywn"—(*Turning card over.*) "Dick is going some where to-night, so I'll come around and go to Mrs. Warrington's with you."

DOUG.   Constance! (*Rising.*) It is my earnest wish that you should not go to the ball to-night. (*Pause.*) I—I am sorry that I am compelled to speak so strongly, but I—I insist.

CONS.   Am I to understand that you command me not to go?

DOUG.   I did not use that word, Constance. I will never use it.   I have too much respect for you to do that.

CONS.   (*Aside.*) · Respect! (*She drops into a chair, her face in her hands, on the back of the chair.   He crosses to her, looking down at her tenderly.*)

DOUG.   Constance—my wife! When we were married, six years ago, in the old church at Concord, as we knelt to receive the blessing of the pastor—your own dear father—a ray of bright sunshine coming through the window fell upon our heads.   For many a month after, that sunlight seemed to rest upon us, and when Rosie came, the pastor's blessing seemed to be fulfilled.   Constance, I—I have tried to be a kind husband to you.

CONS.   A—kind—husband—yes.

DOUG.   And you have been a true, sincere, and devoted wife to me; yet, for the last two years or more, we have been drifting apart further and further.   You speak of compensation in that fashionable world for something that you do not find at home.   Are you likely to find anything there to compensate you for the happiness which you once found here? Does Mrs. Warrington, or Mrs. Maxwell, or Mrs. Dunbar fulfil your idea of a truly happy woman? No, Constance.

CONS.   Mrs. Dunbar is a leader of the circle.

DOUG.   Yes. I believe-she *is* the worst of the set. I am glad to know that you have no personal acquaintance with her.   A woman who respects herself ought to avoid such a person. (*Crosses* R.)

CONS.   That is your opinion of Mrs. Hepworth Dunbar? (*Rising.*)

DOUG.   It is. And I trust that my wife will never be seen in her company. (*Looks at his watch.*) But I am late.   Constance—I—I was wrong to use the word "insist," a moment ago. I feel sure that you will stay at home to-night, not because I "insist," but because it is my earnest—wish. Good night.

CONS. Good night.

DOUGLAS *is moving up* R. CONSTANCE *stands* L. *Enter* BUXTON SCOTT *up* L., *holding a huge package before him.*

SCOTT. (*As he enters.*) Ah! How is the happy mother,—and the father—to-night?

— CONS. and DOUG! Mr. Scott. (*Going to him.*)

SCOTT. Constance! (*Kissing her at one side of package.*) Douglas! (*Looking out at other side of package.*) I haven't a kiss for you.

CONS. Another present for Rosie!

— DOUG. From her godfather.

CONS. Let me help you.

SCOTT. Thank you. (*Putting it on chair* L. C. CONSTANCE *begins to unwrap it.*) I brought that in my arms all the way. I was the proudest old bachelor in New York. I felt like a grandfather.

— DOUG. Constance and I almost feel that you *are* Rosie's grandfather.

CONS. Indeed we do.

SCOTT. So do I. In fact I did have almost as much to do as either of her grandfathers with bringing her into the world. I helped along your courtship as much as a blundering old bachelor could. I patched up your lovers' quarrels and made peace between you—I think I may claim to be Rosie's grandfather. ·

CONS. A beautiful new baby-house, with furniture and carpets and mirrors, complete.—I must kiss you again,—for Rosie. (*Kissing him.*)

SCOTT. I shall drop in to-morrow if I can. You must let me have Douglas now for business. I'm his lawyer, you know, and we lawyers have to work night and day. (*Turns to* DOUGLAS R. C. *apart.*) I must speak with you at once.

— DOUG. (*Apart.*) Come into the library. (*Exeunt up* R.)

CONS. (*Pleasantly.*) I'll not go to Mrs. Warrington's. I'll go to bed early and be up fresh and bright with mother and Edith. Rosie and I will— (*Stops suddenly, her expression changing suddenly from a smile to a look of pain.*) What was that letter from Mrs. Dunbar to my husband? Not a word to me when he read it! (*Pause,* C.) No, no, no! I will not think of that. Douglas has become cold — but—I have never dreamed of anything like that. No!—I—oh! if that, too, should come!—if that, too, should come!—I could not bear it. (*Dropping into a chair,* R. C., *her head falling on her arms.*)

Enter Mrs. DICK CHETWYN, *in full evening dress, up* L.

MRS. DICK. Constance, my dear!

CONS. (*Suddenly arousing herself.*) Ah! Barbara!

MRS. DICK. (*In a tone of great anxiety.*) Something wrong with your new costume, my darling? Doesn't it fit?

CONS. (*Brushing tears from her eyes.*) It is not that.

MRS. DICK. Oh! I thought it was something serious. Your new dress is lovely, and your hair is perfection. Will your husband be ready soon? The men are always late. (*Crosses* C.)

CONS. He is not going this evening.

MRS. DICK. (L. C.) O—h!—that's what you're crying about. It's a long time since I cried because my husband wouldn't go with me anywhere. Dick says I've changed. He says I'm more likely to cry when he does go with me now. Dick goes one way and I go the other, so we're both of us perfectly happy. Buxton Scott called to see Dick one day. I happened to meet him in the hall. "Ah!" said he, "you're at home; of course your husband isn't. Good afternoon." Ha-ha-ha! We two widows must go to the ball by ourselves, I suppose.

CONS. Herbert is going. But didn't you know? Mr. Winthrop is engaged for a supper at the club with your husband. (*Crosses* L., *looking at toys, arranging them, etc.*)

MRS. DICK. Oh! is he? (*Crosses* R.) Ha-ha-ha, I thought Dick was lying about it. He told me he was going to take supper with Mr. Winthrop at the club. After his telling me that, it was the last thing I dreamed of his doing. Poor Dick! it's a shame not to believe him when he does tell the truth; but I dare say they are both lying.

CONS. Oh! Barbara! how can you trifle about such serious things?

MRS. DICK. Well, you see, my dear, I know all about these men, and so'll you by the time you have had two husbands, as I have. My first husband was a physician; my second is a member of the bar. A doctor and a lawyer can teach you about all one woman needs to know on the subject of husbands. Dick makes up whatever Bob omitted in my education, and when I forget anything Bob taught me Dick reminds me of it. Between Bob and Dick together, I'm a graduate—M.A.—Mistress of Arts.

CONS. Ah--I remember—your first husband's name was Robert.

MRS. DICK. M-m. Everybody called me Mrs. Bob then, just as they call me Mrs. Dick now. I never could rise to the dignity of my husband's full name. I dare say next time I shall be Mrs. Jack or Mrs. Tom. Yes, my dear, after you've married the second time, you'll know a great deal too much about these men to worry yourself about 'em. If your dress fits, and you haven't got a headache, no little matrimonial obscurities will ever affect your spirits. Keep your eyes open, my dear, and smile. I mean, keep one eye open and the other shut. When your husband gets round on the blind side of you, open that eye quietly, when he isn't looking. It's great fun! Ha-ha-ha. Bob told me one evening—it was the night of an Arion

ball—no, that wasn't Bob—it was Dick. Dick said to me that
evening—yes, it was Bob, too. It was four years ago—no—
I was a widow then—one, two—(*Counting on her fingers*)—three,
four—that was six years ago. "Barbara, my dear," said Dick
—I mean, said Bob—"I have an important engagement with
a client—no—with a patient—to-night.' '"What sort of a law-
suit is it?" said I—I would say—"What disease is she suffer-
ing from?" said I. Then he quoted from some musty old law-
books—no, he ran over a lot of scientific medical terms.
"Bob," said I, shaking my finger, "it won't do, you can't de-
ceive me, Dick"—Bob—well, it was one of 'em. A woman
that's been the wife of a doctor and a lawyer both gets awfully
mixed up about professional engagements outside of business
hours. (CONSTANCE *has been on her knees before doll-house
arranging furniture, etc.*)

CONS. (*Rises.*) Barbara—I—I don't think I'll go to the ball
to-night.

MRS. DICK. Not go?

CONS. You know, to-morrow is Rosie's birthday. I wish to
be as fresh and as bright as possible to enjoy the whole day
with her. Herbert can go to Mrs. Warrington's with you.

MRS. DICK Well, I've never had any children, but—

CONS. If you had you would feel as I do. Ah, Barbara,
Providence has denied to you the greatest blessing it ever
brings to a woman. Heaven has been very kind to me. (*Turning to house and arranging it.*) I shall not go.

MRS. DICK. You'll break Madam de Battiste's heart if you
don't appear in that costume to-night. Mrs. Dunbar—

CONS. (*Looking up suddenly.*) Mrs. Dunbar! (MRS. DICK
stops and looks at her inquiringly. CONSTANCE *proceeds quietly.*)
What of her?

MRS. DICK. She has a new costume just arrived, direct from
Paris. She is supposed to be the finest dressed woman in
America. But Madam de Battiste told me that when you appeared in the same drawing-room with her to-night, Mrs.
Dunbar and the Parisian dressmakers would lose their reputation. I told Madam de Battiste she might rob the Parisian
dressmakers of their reputation, but Mrs. Hepworth Dunbar will
never lose hers—again. By the by, my dear—ha-ha-ha-ha—
speaking of Mrs. Dunbar—I'm jealous of you.

CONS. Jealous?—of me?

MRS. DICK. M—m. Mrs. Dunbar thinks a great deal more
of your husband than she does of mine. (CONSTANCE *starts to
her feet and moves down* L. C. *front.*) Everybody is talking about
it. Dick was her favorite till a few weeks ago, you know; but
his nose was put out of joint the moment Douglas appeared as
a rival. Ha! ha! ha! We're all laughing at Dick. Ha! ha!
ha! I had such a joke on him last evening. He told me
he was going to drop in and see Mrs. Dunbar. I remarked that
I expected a gentleman to call on me, and he departed with my
blessing. Ha-ha-ha-ha. He was back in twenty minutes.

"Wasn't she in?" said L "Yes," said he, "she was, but just as I reached the foot of the steps Douglas Winthrop was entering the door. I thought I might be intruding. That's the second time this week. When I called on Tuesday I found Winthrop in the parlor." Ha-ha-ha-ha. Your husband has cut mine out. You ought to be proud of him, my dear. The gentleman that was to call upon me—didn't. Dick and I spent the whole evening together. It wasn't so very bad either. It seemed novel to us, you know—we found each other quite interesting.

CONS. (*With suppressed feeling,* L.) You are quite sure that Mrs. Dunbar will be at Mrs. Warrington's this evening.

MRS. DICK. Sure of it. She ordered her costume by cable especially for this occasion.

CONS. (*Aside.*) If she and I should come face to face to-night we would understand each other, without a word. (*Aloud suddenly.*) I will go to Mrs. Warrington's. (*Enter* HERBERT *up* R.) Oh! Herbert, you are ready. Mrs. Chetwyn is going with us. (*Gathering cloak, fan, etc., with nervous movement and speaking rapidly.*) We will send back your carriage, Barbara. Mine has been waiting this half hour. Come. (*Exit quickly and nervously up* L. MRS. DICK *is following her, also* HERBERT, *who is pulling at his back collar-button, working at his wristbands, etc., and looking generally uncomfortable.*)

MRS. DICK. (*Stopping and looking back at* HERBERT.) Herbert!

HER. Mrs. Dick.

MRS. DICK. I know your secret. You're in love. Come here. (*Beckoning to him. He approaches her. She sniffs the air.*) Benzine. Give me your hand. (*He looks at her in some surprise; then holds out his hand. She puts it daintily to her nose.*) Economy—you're very much in love—mended all over —one place with black thread.

HER. I did that myself just now—Aunt Ruth and Edith were both busy.

MRS. DICK. Is Edith busy now?

HER. No.

MRS. DICK. You needn't go with us.

HER. (*Eagerly.*) I needn't?

MRS. DICK. You follow us. I'll leave my carriage at the door for you. We'll give you ten minutes to make love. We'll wait for you in the cloak-room. By-bye—(*going—stops*) Ha-ha-ha—I saw it coming on you three months ago. I'm familiar with the symptoms. I've seen lots of men in love. I married two of 'em. (*Exit up* L.)

HER. Mrs. Dick is a nice woman. (*Looks out* R.) Edith is coming. She has just left little Rosie. I wish she was half as fond of me as she is of Rosie.

Enter EDITH R. 1. E. HERBERT *stands down* L. *beyond table, looking up at her. She touches the doorway lightly, feeling her way ; then moving up* R. C. *until her hand rests upon the back of a chair.*

EDITH. (*To herself.*) I thought the little thing never would go to sleep to-night. Ha-ha-ha—(*laughing lightly.*) She is so excited about her birthday. Now I can finish her present. (*She crosses, touching another chair lightly on the way and moves to table* L. C., *taking up a little lace bed-spread.*)

—HER. (*As she is crossing.*) She is smiling. Edith is always happy.

EDITH. (*Standing at right of table and facing* HERBERT *and sewing.*) I wonder what Herbert is doing now?

—HER. (*Aside.*) What pretty eyes she has !

EDITH. I always feel a little lonely when Herbert is away.

—HER. (*Aside.*) I wonder what she is thinking about.

EDITH. (*Listening suddenly and smiling.*) There's some one here. (*Laughing lightly and holding out her hand.*) Let me guess. (HERBERT *reaches forward his hand and touches the back of her hand gently with one finger.*) Herbert!—(*pleased*)—I thought you had gone to the ball.

—HER. How do you always know when *I* touch your hand, Edith ?

EDITH. Something tells me, Herbert.

HER. Something tells you?

EDITH. I seem to feel that it is you. Your touch is always so different from the others. It seems so—so gentle—and so—

HER. So—tender—and—and—loving ?

EDITH. Yes, Herbert.

—HER. I do love you, Edith.

EDITH. I'm glad of that, Herbert. I like to have you all love me.

HER. Yes—of course, but—the others you know—we all love you—certainly—but the rest of them—it's different with me. (*A slight pause as if waiting for her to speak.*) The rest of them—except Douglas, they're women, you know—and little Rosie.

EDITH. Well, can't they love me just as well as you ?

HER. Yes—they—of course they can love you as well as I —but—my love is a different kind of love from theirs.

EDITH. What do you mean—different—Herbert ? (*She sits* L. C.)

—HER. (*Aside.*) It's no use. I can't make love to her. (*Aloud.*) Ask Aunt Ruth what the difference is, Edith. Is that a present for Rosie?

EDITH. Yes. (*Breaking thread, etc.*) It is just finished. A little lace spread for the doll's bedstead her papa bought.

_ HER. It is very pretty. I am going to take a holiday to-morrow, and spend the whole day with you and Rosie.

EDITH. Oh ! I'm so glad. You are very fond of Rosie.

—HER. Yes, I'm very fond, indeed, of—Rosie.

EDITH. You spend all the time you can with her and me.

Her. Yes—with her—and—and—you.

Edith. What long soft hair Rosie has—and her face is as smooth as a peach, and it's as sweet too. She is beautiful.

Her. You see so many beautiful things, Edith! You never wish that you could see with your eyes, do you?

Edith. Why should I? No, indeed! I am always happy —like everybody else in the world. I sometimes dream, Herbert that there are people who are not happy. I dream that people are sometimes unkind to each other. Of course, I know it is only a dream; for when I wake up everybody is so gentle and good, and so happy; but something whispers to me it is better to be as I am. I do not wish to see.

Her. We all have eyes for you, Edith; even little Rosie—

Edith. Oh! Rosie's eyes are mine. She leads me about everywhere and tells me of everything, all day long.

Her. I wish I could lead you around everywhere, as Rosie does. (Crosses c.)

Edith. You are not always with me.

Her. I would like to be with you always.

Edith. Would you, Herbert?

Her. Edith—I—I hope to have a little home of my own some day.

Edith. A home of your own? Do you mean—you—you will go away from here?

Her. Why—yes—I—I—I hope to have—a—wife.

Edith. Wife! Oh! Herbert! (With warm feeling putting her arms about his neck.) You must never leave us.

Her. Leave you? no—I—I don't want to leave you.

Edith. Oh—can Rosie and I go with you to your little home? (Sitting L. C.)

Her. Well—you—of course, if—if Rosie—but—you—see— when a young man gets married—I—I love Rosie very much— but—you—she—we—you'd better ask Aunt Ruth about that, too, Edith. I must go now. Good night.

Edith. Good night, Herbert. (Reaching up her face for him to kiss her. He leans down, about to kiss her lips; he hesitates, then raises her hand and kisses it gently.)

Her. Good night. (Exit up L.)

Edith. (Aside) Herbert will never be lonely in his little home with so many of us; but I—I—I wish that other one wouldn't be there.

(Enter Mrs. Ruth R. 1. E. and crosses to Edith.) It is long after bed-time, my darling. If Rosie should wake up she would miss you. You have finished the spread, I see. (Taking spread from Edith, who sits in deep thought.) It is very nicely done, my dear.

Edith. Mother?

Mrs. Ruth. Edith.

Edith. What—different kinds—(rising)—of love—are there?

Mrs. Ruth. Different kinds of love? There are many kinds, my pet: a mother's love; a father's, or a sister's, or brother's, or a friend's. Then there's another love, Edith—the love that two good people have for each other when they are married.

EDITH. Do two people always get married when they love each other?

MRS. RUTH. Not always. They generally do.

EDITH. Why?

MRS. RUTH. They feel lonely. They want to be together —to comfort and to take care of each other. But you mustn't sit up any longer. (*Walking with her* R.) I'll come to you as soon as I arrange the little bedstead. (EDITH *goes out* R. 1. E.) I have given the little pet her first lesson in love. (*Looking after her.*) That's quite enough for the present, I think. (*Turning and crossing up* L.) Herbert does need a little help. (*Kneeling at a toy bedstead, arranging spread, etc.* EDITH *is heard calling "Mother" without.* MRS. RUTH *starts up. Re-enter* EDITH.)

EDITH. Mother! oh! mother! (*Rushing across stage excitedly.*)

MRS. RUTH. (*Intercepting her* L. C.) My child.

EDITH. Rosie! Rosie! She is not asleep—nor awake—she is struggling—and—

MRS. RUTH. Calm yourself, my child. Rosie is dreaming, perhaps. She has been so excited all day.

EDITH. She is so cold and she breathes so hard.

MRS. RUTH. Come, Edith. (*She goes out with* EDITH R. 1. E.)

Enter BUXTON SCOTT *and* DOUGLAS, *up* R.

SCOTT. (*As he enters and passes across* L.) That's the only obstacle in our way now, DOUGLAS. The directors of the bank are willing to settle it.

DOUG. (*Crossing down to table* L. C.) I'll do all I can in the matter.

SCOTT. See you in the morning. (*Waving his hand.*)

DOUG. (*Waving his hand.*) At nine. (*Exit* SCOTT *up* L. DOUGLAS *takes note from his pocket.*) What hour did she say? (*Reads.*) "Any time before eleven." I must send a line to CHETWYN (*writes*), and tell him it is impossible for me to join him at supper this evening. (*Strikes bell. Enter* MAID *up* L. DOUGLAS *encloses note in envelope, directs it, and rises. Goes up and hands note to* MAID.) Tell Morgan to take this to the Union Club—immediately. (*Exit* MAID. *He looks at his watch.*) Now for Mrs. Dunbar's. (*Exit up* L.)

CURTAIN.

ACT SECOND.

SCENE—*The Same. Night. A single lamp or drop-light
upon table. At rise of curtain enter* DOUGLAS *up* L., *in
some haste, and with expression of anxiety. He is still in
evening dress and has his overcoat on his arm and hat in
hand, as if having entered too hastily to throw them aside.
He tosses them on chair as he proceeds. He is followed by*
MAID.

DOUG. *(As he crosses* C.*)* Eleven o'clock, you say?

MAID. Yes, sir. Miss Rosie was taken ill about the time
you left the house, sir.

DOUG. Did Dr. Mellbanke come promptly?

MAID. Yes, sir. And he is still here.

DOUG. Still here! *(Looks at his watch.)* Two o'clock. Dr.
Mellbanke still here. It must be serious. *(Going quickly
down* R. DR. MELLBANKE *steps in* R. 1 E., *raising his hand
to check him.)* The child, Doctor!—Rosie!

DOCTOR. She is sleeping.

DOUG. Is there danger?

DOCTOR. I hope for the best.

DOUG. Ah! *(With a sigh of relief, walking* L.*)* What is it,
Doctor? *(The* MAID *goes out, with coat and hat.)*

DOCTOR. Just such an attack as she had two years ago.

DOUG. She recovered from that in a few days.

DOCTOR. I trust she will do the same in this case.

DOUG. Has she suffered much?

DOCTOR. She is now entirely free from pain.

DOUG. Can I go to the room, Doctor?

DOCTOR. She is in a quiet sleep. We must take every ad-
vantage of it.

DOUG. I might relieve her mother.

DOCTOR. The child's grandmother is with her.

DOUG. Ah—Constance is resting.

DOCTOR. Mrs. Winthrop, herself, has not returned yet.

DOUG. Not—returned?

DOCTOR. She is at Mrs.—Warrington's—I believe.

DOUG. *(With a slight start.)* At Mrs. Warrington's?

DOCTOR. Up to half an hour ago I thought the case a very
harmless one, and I advised them not to send for Mrs.
Winthrop. But it took a more serious turn, and we sent for
her. She has not arrived yet.

DOUG. *(Aside.)* Constance did go!

DOCTOR. I thought it was she that entered, when I heard
you at the door. I came down stairs to ask her not to go to
the child at present. Mrs. Winthrop will be somewhat ex-

cited of course—returning from a—a social festivity—under such—such unusual circumstances.

DOUG. Yes. (*With some bitterness in his tone.*) From a fashionable ball-room to the bedside of a sick child is an abrupt change—for a mother.

DOCTOR. Will you kindly say to Mrs. Winthrop, for me, when she arrives, that the little one is sleeping and the utmost quiet is necessary. Her grandmother is taking every care of her. If Mrs. Winthrop will, for the present, kindly refrain from coming to the room--

DOUG. I will tell her.

DOCTOR. It will be better for the child. (*Exit* R. 1 E.)

DOUG. Better for the child!—that its mother should not enter it's sick-room in a rustling silk and a dragging train—fresh from the glare of a ball-room.

Enter MRS. RUTH R. 1 E.

MRS. RUTH. (R. C.) Douglas.

DOUG. (R. C.) Mother. Rosie is still sleeping?

MRS. RUTH. Yes, gently, and without pain. The Doctor is with her now. I am glad the servant found you, Douglas. We sent to the club for you, at first.

DOUG. I was not there. How—how did you know where I was, mother?

MRS. RUTH. I happened to overhear you say to Mr. Scott that you would go to—to a Mrs.—a Mrs. Dunbar's.

DOUG. Ah! yes, I see.

MRS. RUTH. When the servant returned and said you were not at the club, I thought you might be at that lady's house, so Dr. Mellbanke sent there for you.

DOUG. Mother—I—I have a—a favor to ask of you. Say nothing to Constance about my having been at Mrs. Dunbar's to-night.

MRS. RUTH. Say—nothing—to—Constance! My son!

DOUG. Do not misunderstand me, mother.

MRS. RUTH. No, Douglas!—of course not. I heard Mr. Scott, tell you that it was positively necessary for you to go to Mrs. Dunbar's—some business matter.

DOUG. Yes, mother, it was, and the cause of my going would bring deep pain to Constance, something, indeed, harder to bear than mere pain.

MRS. RUTH. Nothing can be so important, Douglas, as perfect confidence between husband and wife.

DOUG. Mother, *please* do not say anything on this subject to her.

MRS. RUTH. Well, I—I promise you. I would not have mentioned it any way. Constance should have returned by this time.

DOUG. It is too early, yet, to leave the most brilliant reception of the season.

MRS. RUTH.   Early?—with such a message?   What do you mean, Douglas?

Enter MAID *up* L.

MAID.   Thomas is returned, madam.

MRS. RUTH.   And Mrs. Winthrop?

MAID.   Mrs. Winthrop had left the house before Thomas got there, madam.

MRS. RUTH.   Ah.   She has taken Mrs. Chetwyn home.

(*Exit* MAID.)

DOUG.   They are discussing the merits of the last new costumes.   (*Sitting* L. C.)

MRS. RUTH.   Douglas, I—I never heard you speak of your wife in a bitter tone.

DOUG.   My—wife—went to a "fashionable" woman's house, to-night, against the earnestly expressed desire of her husband.   She is now away from her sick child.   The physician has just requested me to ask her not to go to its bedside when she returns.   I am a husband and a father!   Do you wonder at my bitter tone?

MRS. RUTH.   (*After a moment's pause.*)   Douglas—my son.

DOUG.   Mother.   (*She crosses to him and stands at his chair, looking down at him.*)

MRS. RUTH.   May I speak frankly to you?

DOUG.   Need *you* ask me that?

MRS. RUTH.   Even a mother fears to touch upon some subjects.   I have long wished to say what is in my heart, but I—I have hesitated.

DOUG.   It *must* be good for me to know all there is in such a heart as yours.   (*Taking her hand.*)   Through childhood and manhood I have never found anything but love there.

MRS. RUTH.   My darling boy!

DOUG.   I am a boy again, mother.   Speak to me—just as you used to.   (*He has placed her in the chair and is sitting on a stool beside her.*)

MRS. RUTH.   I—I feel to-night, Douglas, that a crisis may be at hand, in the life of the two beings most dear to me in all the world.   You are my only child—no!—my only *son*—for *she* too is my child—my daughter.   I have known Constance since she was a little girl.   I know how pure—how full of tenderness and love—her nature is.   You were very happy—at first.

DOUG.   Very—at first.

MRS. RUTH.   There was contentment and love in your home.   A change has been gradually stealing over you both.

DOUG.—Yes, mother!—a change.

MRS. RUTH.   Constance has become more and more what is called a "fashionable" woman.

DOUG.   Yes.

MRS. RUTH.   Her child and her husband do not, now, receive all her attention, as they once did.

DOUG.   No.

MRS. RUTH.   Her home has become less and less the centre of her thoughts.

Doug. My dear mother!—*Speak* to Constance. A single word from you—

Mrs. Ruth. No—my son—it is to you that I will speak !

Doug. To—me?

Mrs. Ruth. It is your fault, Douglas, not hers. If such a woman as Constance is not the wife and mother she should be, it is her husband's fault.

Doug. My—fault ! (*Rising and crossing* c.)

Mrs. Ruth. (*After a slight pause, assuming a lighter tone.*) You did not dine at home this evening, Douglas. You dropped in at Delmonico's with a friend, you told me.

Doug. (*After looking up at her as if a little puzzled at the change of subject.*) Yes!—we had a matter of business to talk over.

Mrs. Ruth. You were absent from home all *yesterday* evening.

~~Doug. A private meeting of our Board of Directors.~~

Mrs. Ruth. You had a gentleman's dinner-party here on *Tuesday* evening.

~~Doug. Some capitalists to meet the president of a western railroad.~~

Mrs. Ruth. You—you never return to your home in the daytime.

Doug. Business men never do that. (*Crosses* R. C.) We lunch down-town, of course.

~~Mrs. Ruth. Of course. On Monday evening—~~

~~Doug. I was over to Philadelphia, Monday afternoon—a large contract for railroad iron. (*Sitting* R. C.)~~

Mrs. Ruth. (*Rises and crosses to him.*) I have now been here two months, Douglas. Your wife never sees you in the daytime, except on Sunday ; and only three times since I came have you spent an evening quietly at home with her.

Doug. The constant pressure upon the time of a business man—

Mrs. Ruth. Your *father* was a business man, Douglas! a successful one, too. He left you a large fortune, but he made *me* a very happy wife. *He* never forgot that his wife and child were more to him than all the triumphs of his business life. Remember your own childhood. Remember the many happy hours your father spent with you and me in our home. The trials of his daily work never made those hours less bright. Even your father's *successes* in business did not conflict with our domestic happiness.

Doug. Those times were different, mother.

Mrs. Ruth. No, my son ! Domestic love in those days withered and died in the same hot fever as now. *You* have caught the disease and your father *escaped* it—that is all. Believe me, there are as many men to-day as then, rich and successful men, who do not neglect their families for the sake of making "money"—who do not sacrifice their wives and their children and all their own holiest affections—

Doug. Sacrifice!

Mrs. Ruth. Yes, Douglas, sacrifice!—

Doug. Surely you do not think that I—

Mrs. Ruth. That is what *you* are *doing*, my son. Your wife has become almost a stranger to you. Her heart is slowly starving for want of your love. She is turning in her loneliness to the excitements of fashionable life. What effect *must* this daily separation have upon a woman like Constance? (*Goes up* C.) You have given her a magnificent house to live in, but you've given her no home.

Doug. Mother!

Mrs. Ruth. For months you and she have been growing colder to each other every day.

Doug. Colder and colder—yes.

Mrs. Ruth. Now— (*She hesitates.*)

Doug. Now—well?

Mrs. Ruth. Your child alone holds you together.

Doug. Our child! If she were to be taken away—!

Mrs. Ruth. Then, Douglas, the holy grief of a father and mother would bring you and Constance together. If that great sorrow were ever to come upon you, it would bring its compensation. Two hearts never know all there is of love until they have *suffered* together.

Doug. (*After a pause, and holding her hand in both his own.*) This same kind hand that led me when I was a boy shall lead me now, mother. (*Rising.*) I have been cruel to Constance. She shall not be without a home hereafter. I will be her companion—her husband! As soon as she returns I will confess the wrong I have done her. Our love shall have a new and a stronger life than ever—from this night.

Mrs. Ruth. When you speak like that I seem to hear your father's own voice.

Doug. (*Walking* R. *with her, his arm about her waist.*) I will try to honor his memory by making Constance as happy a wife as he made you. We shall both bless *you* for it, mother!

Mrs. Ruth. My boy! (*Reaching up her face. He kisses her Exit* Mrs. Ruth, R. 1 E.

Doug. (*Looking after her.*) "Her children arise up and call her blessed." (*Exit after her,* R. 1 E. *A moment's pause the stage empty.*)

Enter Constance, *up* L.

Cons. Back again! (*With a weary air, throwing aside her cloak.*) How quiet the house is! It's no use going to bed; I cannot sleep. (*Dropping into chair before fire,* R.) I wish these "social gayeties," as they call them, could go on forever. No matter how much I go out, or how bright the company is, it always ends in this; I am alone again, and I—I can't stop thinking. Oh!—I wish I *could*—I *wish* I could! (*Looks into fire.*) Mr. Chetwyn was at the reception this evening;

Douglas sent him word he could not meet him at the club.
He sent the message after receiving that note from Mrs. Dunbar—*she* was *not* there to-night! Oh!—why must I keep
thinking—thinking? (*Starting to her feet and moving* C.,
pauses.) Perhaps I am wronging him. Yes. No—no!—I
will *not* believe it—I *have* not lost his love! There is something I do not understand. I will speak to Douglas about it
in the morning. (*Smiling.*) It will all come right. I must
get to sleep as soon as I can, to be up bright and early with
Rosie. I will peep in at my little darling before I go to sleep.
· (*Going toward door,* R. 1 E.)

Enter EDITH, R. 1 E.; *also* HERBERT; *up* L.

CONS. Edith!
EDITH. Oh, Constance! you have come back.
CONS. Why are *you* up at this hour?
EDITH. I couldn't sleep. They told me to go to my room.
But I was so unhappy about Rosie—
CONS. Rosie!
EDITH. Oh!—you do not know?
CONS. Know what, Edith!—I do not know what?
EDITH. The servant was sent to tell you—he—
CONS. Ah! (*A half-suppressed scream.*) Rosie!—Rosie!
She is not well! (*She hurries past* EDITH *and out* R. 1 E.
under great excitement.)
HER. (*Joining* EDITH *up* R. C.) The servant must have
missed us, Edith. What is it?
EDITH. Rosie is ill. The doctor is here. They sent me
away.

Re-enter MRS. RUTH *with* CONSTANCE, R. 1 E. MRS. RUTH *is
leading her in, holding one of* CONSTANCE'S *hands, and her
arm about her waist.* CONSTANCE *is under great emotion.*

MRS. RUTH. You *must* calm yourself, my dear child. You
must *calm* yourself! Dr. Mellbanke is right.
CONS. Yes—I know—I know. (*Moving up* L. C.)
MRS. RUTH. (C.) You shall go to her, presently. But she
is sleeping very quietly. The slightest noise might—
CONS. The doctor is right—he is right. I *am* excited! I
have just returned from where people are dancing and
laughing. I would endanger the life of my child! (*Sinking into chair at table,* R. C.) My own child! Douglas—
my husband! ask *him* to come to me, mother; ask him to
come to me.
MRS. RUTH. I will—I will.
CONS. Tell Douglas I want him near me—I want his arm
about me, mother.
MRS. RUTH. Whatever happens, trust to *his* love. It will
always support and comfort you!—my daughter! (*Kissing
her; she then turns to* HERBERT, C., *speaking apart.*) Herbert, Dr. Mellbanke wishes you to go for Dr. Holden—at once.

HER. (*Apart.*) A consultation!

MRS. RUTH. H-s-h. (*Her finger to her lips.*) Dr. Mellbanke wishes to advise with him. (HERBERT *turns up stage and exit* L. MRS. RUTH *crosses* R.) I will speak to Douglas, Constance (*Exit* R. 1 E.)

CONS. (*Taking off her jewels, etc., nervously, and dropping them on the table before her.*) Oh, how I *hate* them! How I hate them! Why did I go to-night? My husband!—I never longed for your love as I do now.

(EDITH *makes her way across to* CONSTANCE.)

EDITH. Constance. (*Laying her hand on her shoulder.*)

CONS. Edith—sister!

EDITH. I am glad you have come back. Rosie was talking to me about you before she fell asleep.

CONS. *You* have been where *I* should have been to-night. (*Taking* EDITH'S *hand and kissing it.* EDITH *starts slightly and puts her other hand to* CONSTANCE'S *cheek.*) What did Rosie say, Edith?

EDITH. You are crying, Constance. (*Sinking to her knees beside her, with her arms about her.*) Don't cry. The last word Rosie said, before she fell asleep, was—"Mamma." She loves you very much. She often, often tells me so. Don't cry, Constance.

CONS. Did her papa come home before she went to sleep?

EDITH. No. Mother sent to the club for him, at first, but he was not there. It took a long time to send to the other place, and Rosie was asleep when he came.

CONS. The—the other place;—where?

EDITH. To—to some lady's house

CONS. Some—some lady's—house?

EDITH. I forget the name—but you would know—Mrs.— Mrs.— Dun— Dun—

CONS. Dunbar!

EDITH. Yes—that's the name.

CONS. Mother—sent—to see if—if Douglas was at—at Mrs. Dunbar's?

EDITH. Yes. Fortunately he *was* there. I'm so glad you have both come back. It seems as if you *ought* to be together to-night. Don't cry, Constance. (*Reaching up with her arms about* CONSTANCE'S *neck, as the latter sits rigidly looking away.*) Rosie will be so glad to see you when she wakes up. The Doctor says she will soon get well. (*Her voice breaking as she speaks, and finally dropping her head into* CONSTANCE'S *lap, weeping.*) Don't cry.

CONS. You must go to bed, Edith, at once. (*Rising with arm about* EDITH *and leading her up* R., *almost choking as she speaks, but controlling herself by an effort.*) It is after two o'clock.

EDITH. Oh, I cannot sleep, Constance—I cannot sleep. Do not send me away.

CONS. You—you must go to your room, Edith.

EDITH.   If you wish it, Constance.

CONS.   Yes; good night.

EDITH.   Good night.   (*Kissing each other.   Exit* EDITH *up*
R.   CONSTANCE *moves down and across* L; *supports herself
by a chair* L. C.)

CONS.   I—I cannot breathe—I—it is growing dark!—I—
Douglas—my husband!—my heart is breaking! (*Burying her
face in her hands.*)

Enter DOUGLAS R. 1 E.

DOUG.   Constance— (*Sees her emotion and crosses to her rapidly.*)   My dear Constance!   You are unstrung by this sudden
news.   You are nervous.   Be seated.   (*She drops into the
chair.*)   Command yourself, my darling.

CONS.   Yes—(*drawing up rigidly*)—I—I *will* command myself.

DOUG.   Let us hope for the best.   Dr. Mellbanke says that
Rosie may awake from from her sleep refreshed and on the
road to recovery.

CONS.   (*Aside.*)   Summoned from that woman's house to the
bedside of his sick child!

DOUG.   This night will be the beginning of a new and a
happy life for you and me, Constance—the beginning of a
deeper and stronger love than we have ever known before.
Rosie's future will be all the brighter for it.   I have not been
such a husband to you, of late years, as I ought.   My feverish
haste to make a larger fortune has led to what has seemed to
you neglect;—and it was none the less neglect because I was
unconscious of it.   I have allowed business considerations to
outweigh all that is best in a man's life.

CONS.   (*Aside.*)   Business considerations! (*Rising.*)

DOUG.   Our love has been only flickering.   It has not died
out.   We will be companions hereafter.

CONS.   (*Aside.*)   Companions!

DOUG.   You do not answer me, Constance. (*A pause.   She
maintains her silence rigidly, looking away from him.*)   You are
still silent? (DOUGLAS *stands looking at her a moment, and
then crosses* R. C. *s'owly.   He stops and looks down in thought.*)
Have I discovered my fault too late?

CONS.   At that woman's house!

(DR. MELLBANKE *enters* R. 1 E., *and stops, looks first at* CON-
STANCE, *then at* DOUGLAS.   *The latter turns to speak.*)

DOUG.   Constance—my—wife—I— (DR. MELLBANKE *ad-
vances, taps him on the shoulder, and beckons to him quietly.*
DOUGLAS *starts and stops, as if a sudden fear checked him.*
DR. MELLBANKE *glances at* CONSTANCE *and motions silence on
his lips.*   DOUGLAS *starts with a short, quick breath.*   CONSTANCE
turns suddenly at the sound, and looks at them both.   The DOC-
TOR *beckons to* DOUGLAS *out of room, quietly takes his arm and
walks out with him* R. 1 E.   CONSTANCE *wavers a moment on her*

*feet ; then gives a quick, sharp scream, as if suddenly comprehend-
ing the truth. She staggers across right, front, trying to reach
door at* R. 1 E. Douglas *reappears.)*

CONS. Rosie—not—not—

DOUG. Be—be strong, my darling—be strong!

CONS. Rosie is—she is— (*Staggering.* DOUGLAS *supports
her.*)

DOUG. It—is—over. (*She sinks into the chair, at table.
He stands over her, looking down tenderly.*) She passed away
in her sleep. My wife! (*Bends down as if to embrace her. She
looks up into his face with a cold, half-dazed expression, then
turns from him and sinks with her head upon her arms.*
DOUGLAS *withdraws from her slowly, then speaks.*) The last—
link—broken!

CURTAIN.

ACT THIRD.

SCENE—*Drawing-room. Door up* R. *with hall or another apart-
ment at back. Door* R. 1 E. *Discovered :* CONSTANCE *sitting* L. C., *and* EDITH *on a low stool by her side.* CONSTANCE
is dressed in black ; EDITH *in white, trimmed with black.*

EDITH. I have been thinking about Douglas and you, Constance, almost all the time, to-day and yesterday. I dreamed
about you last night. It seems very, very sad for Douglas to
go away to Europe to-day—all by himself.

CONS. Yes, Edith ; it *is* sad.

EDITH. He will be very lonely ; and you will be lonely, too.
Why don't you go with him ?

CONS. Go with him ? Why—I—never mind, my pet. Do not
trouble your dear little head about Douglas and me. We—we
do not find it convenient—to go together.

EDITH. How long will Douglas be gone ?

CONS. I—I cannot tell.

EDITH. When I asked him, he said *he* didn't know.

CONS. Don't think of it, darling.

EDITH. I can't help it ; I love you both so dearly, and I
don't wish you to be unhappy. Mother told me that two
people who loved each other enough to be married wished always to be together ; and I know how I should feel if some one
that I loved like that should go away.

CONS. Some one you loved ?

EDITH. Love holds two people together so closely, that one is wretched without the other.

CONS. Why, my little innocent! How did *you* come to know anything of *that?*

EDITH. I—I don't know; I—I've been thinking about it for a long time. Sometimes I ask Mother. She always tells me to listen to my own heart. I—I *have* been listening to it. I—I *do* love some one, Constance! (*Dropping her head into* CONSTANCE'S *lap*).

CONS. My child!

EDITH. I'm not a child any longer, sister.

CONS. I *see* you are not, my dear.

Enter HERBERT, *up* R.

HER. Edith! (EDITH *starts up, rising and looking down with "consciousness" in her manner.*) I've come up to go to the steamer with Uncle Douglas. Here's a bunch of violets. They're the first of the season; I've been watching for them.

EDITH. Oh! thank you.

HER. It's half an hour yet before Douglas will go; and you are so fond of flowers—wouldn't you like to go into the conservatory?

EDITH. Yes, Herbert. (*He is leading her up. After a few steps she returns and leans over* CONSTANCE, *who still sits down* L. C.) Sister, *don't* let Douglas go alone!

CONS. (*Kissing her.*) Go with Herbert, my darling.

(EDITH *turns to* HERBERT, *who leads her up and out* R.) No longer a child! I hope she will be happy.

Enter MAID *with card, up* R.

(*Reading card.*) "Mrs. Robert W. Mackenzie." (*Aside.*) One of mother's friends, I suppose—from Boston, perhaps. (*Aloud.*) Take the card to Mrs. Winthrop, Jeanette.

(*Exit* MAID, L. 1 E. *Enter* MRS. DICK, *up* R. Barbara!

MRS. DICK. Constance, my love! Your husband is going to Europe, to-day, I hear.

CONS. Yes. (*Crossing* R. *and sitting.*)

MRS. DICK. (C.) Business, I suppose. A married man never seems to care for the distance he has to travel—on business—when he's alone. Dick told me one day—there was a big law-case in the West—no, that was Bob—it was a medical convention. "I've got to go to Chicago, my dear, on professional business," said he. "Oh, how *far!*" said I. "Merely a pleasant jaunt," said he. "*I'll* go *with* you, my love," said I. "My darling," said he, "it's *nine hundred miles!*" Ha-ha-ha-ha! First class in matrimonial geography: What is the exact distance between the city of New York and the city of Chicago? Answer: It depends on circumstances. Correct; go to the head. (*Enter* MRS. RUTH, L. 1 E., *the card in her hand.*) Ah!

my dear Mrs. Winthrop, I came to tell Constance some news—
you shall hear it, too.

MRS. RUTH. Thank you; I shall be very glad. But—(*looking across to* CONSTANCE)—you sent me a card, Constance—a Mrs. Mackenzie.

CONS. She is in the reception-room. Isn't she calling on you?

MRS. DICK. Why, *I'm* Mrs. Mackenzie!

CONS. You!

MRS. DICK. That's *my* card.

MRS. RUTH. (*Confused.*) But—your name—is—Chetwyn.

MRS. DICK. It was day before yesterday. Dick and I have got a divorce.

CONS. A divorce!

MRS. RUTH. Divorce!

MRS. DICK. M—m. That's my news. Sit down. I'll tell you all about it. (*They sit.*) We've been living in Connecticut for the last year, you know—except a few months in New York, during the winter.

CONS. Yes—I know.

MRS. RUTH. (*With a bewildered air.*) What has living in Connecticut to do with a—a divorce?

MRS. DICK. It has everything to do with it. They grant you a divorce there for incompatibility of temper.

MRS. RUTH. But I—I didn't know that you and your husband were incompatible.

MRS. DICK. Neither did *we*—till we went to live in Connecticut. We never knew we *had* any tempers, to speak of, before. When we took a house in Stamford, we didn't dream of the effect it would have on a man and wife. Of course Dick and I were both witnesses in the case.

MRS. RUTH. It must have been very sad.

MRS. DICK. Yes, it was:—I had on a brocade—lavender and old gold—lace to match the lavender—and sleeves puffed above the elbows. (MRS. RUTH *looks at her in bewilderment.*) The evidence was so comical.

MRS. RUTH. Comical!

MRS. DICK. You ought to have been there. Ha-ha-ha-ha! It was all about how Dick and I have been saying things to each other for a year—so as to obey the laws of the State. We called each other all sorts o' names. When we were first married Dick said I was a turtle-dove;—after we got to Connecticut he said I was a snapping turtle-dove. Ha-ha-ha-ha! I began by calling him a donkey—and then I called him a whole lot of other animals. He told the judge, according to me he was a regular Noah's Ark. I told the judge Dick called *me* animals too. The judge said we seemed to be a happy family; —and so he granted the divorce. I've gone back to my first husband's name.

CONS. Ah—I remember:—Mackenzie.

MRS. DICK. I'm Mrs. Bob, again now. I gave Dick all the

old cards I had left over—and the plate. I didn't want to keep Dick's name. If he should get married again, it'd be awkward, having two of us; we'd get mixed up. Of course it doesn't make any difference to Bob. So Douglas sails to-day.

MRS. RUTH. (*Rising.*) Yes !—and if you will kindly excuse me—

MRS. DICK. Certainly. (*Rising.*) I must run along, myself. Good morning.

MRS. RUTH. Good morning. (*Then moving to her and speaking very earnestly.*) Believe me, my dear Mrs.—Mrs.—

MRS. DICK. Mackenzie.

MRS. RUTH. Mackenzie. I am very sorry that you and your husband are separated.

MRS. DICK. (*Earnestly.*) Thank you, my dear Mrs. Winthrop—but don't worry yourself about it :—*we* don't. (MRS. RUTH *turns, throwing up her hands, and goes out* L., *shaking her head.*) Good by, Constance, my love—I'm going to pop in and tell Mrs. Garnette :—she's just got a divorce, too, you know. (*Kissing her and running up stage.*)

CONS. Good by. (*Moving up into recess of window* L. *and stands looking out.*)

MRS. DICK. (*Stopping up* R. C. *near opening, and looking* R.) Here's Mr. Buxton Scott. (BUXTON SCOTT *appears from* R. *He and* MRS. DICK *bow deeply to each other.*)

SCOTT. Mrs. Chetwyn.

MRS. DICK. Mrs.—Mackenzie !—if you please.

SCOTT. (*Turning and looking after her.*) Eh ?—Mac?- -

MRS. DICK. Dick and I are separated.

SCOTT. I never happened to meet either of you when you *weren't* separated.

MRS. DICK. We've got a divorce.

SCOTT. Ah ! Then you and Dick will *see* something of each other. I congratulate you both. When were you divorced ?

MRS. DICK. Day before yesterday.

SCOTT. And you've married a Mr. Mackenzie since ?

MRS. DICK. Mr. Scott !

SCOTT. Oh ! I beg your pardon; you've taken your first husband's name ?

MRS. DICK. Yes. My maiden name was too far back. By the by, my darling old aunt, Miss Vandevere, said the other day that she hoped you would come and see her.

SCOTT. With pleasure. She's a charming old lady. Give her my compliments. Tell her I hope to drop in often.

MRS. DICK. I will. I'm living with her.

SCOTT. Eh ? (*In surprise and turning* L.)

MRS. DICK. You are still a bachelor ?

SCOTT. I am.

MRS. DICK. I pity you, Mr. Scott. You should marry.

SCOTT. And pity myself ? I prefer to have *you* pity me.

MRS. DICK. (*Approaching him.*) You really ought to make some woman happy.

SCOTT. (*Aside.*) She's after number three. (*Turning to her.*) My dear Mrs. Dick.

MRS. DICK. Bob.

SCOTT. Mrs. Bob. (*Looking down at her through his eyeglasses.*) I'll drop in on Dick and ask *his* opinion.. He knows you *so* well.

MRS. DICK. Me! Bless you! I meant Aunt Jane.

SCOTT. Oh! (*Turning L.*)

MRS. DICK. I'm sure she'd make you happy. She's a charming old lady. Ha-ha-ha-ha—(*Running R.—stops.*) Come and see Aunt Jane—often. (*Exit up R.*)

SCOTT. An old maid and a young grass widow! Two to one! (*Crossing R.*) I shall not call. (*He turns, changing his tone and manner.*) Constance. (*She turns to him, giving both her hands. He holds them in his own, looking at her with kindly interest, and speaking in an earnest, fatherly tone.*) Douglas asked me to come and see him this morning, before he sailed.

CONS. He is in his room. I will send for him.

SCOTT. Thank you. (*He still retains her hands, looking steadily into her face.*) Constance, I have known you and Douglas since you were children. You have often called me your "second father."

CONS. You are the dearest friend we have in the world.

SCOTT. There is something on your heart.

CONS. On—my—heart?

SCOTT. I'm only a hard old bachelor, and a stony-hearted old lawyer, but you may speak to me—as—as if I were really your father.

CONS. There are some things which one cannot—*will* not—talk about—to *any* one.

SCOTT. When you were a little girl, you used to bring all your troubles to me.

CONS. I am a woman now.

SCOTT. Constance, there is something wrong between you and your husband.

CONS. Something—wrong!—yes.

SCOTT. Will you confide in me?

CONS. I—I—(*hesitates—turns away*)—oh! I cannot!—I cannot confide in *any* one.

SCOTT. I will not ask you to; but I will give you the advice which your own father would give if he were living. Whatever is on your heart, go to your husband—

CONS. To *him*!—no, I am a humiliated wife. My natural pride compels me to be silent.

SCOTT. What can have happened to make you feel like this?

CONS. We will not talk about that. For two years and over we have been growing more distant and more indifferent. I am worn out, with such a life, at last. We—we do not love each other now.

SCOTT. M—m—m. You do not love each other?

CONS. No; our love is a matter of the past.

SCOTT. How long will Douglas be gone?

CONS. I—I do not know.

SCOTT. M—m—m. Of course, now that your love is a matter of the past (*glancing at her shrewdly*), it must be a great relief to you to—to have Douglas go away.

CONS. Yes,—it is—(*choking*)—a—a—a great relief. (*Bursting into tears.* SCOTT *approaches her and drops one arm about her waist.*)

SCOTT. My child!

CONS. Father! (*Turning to him and hiding her face in his breast.*)

SCOTT. (*Tenderly, yet half humorously, patting her head.*) I'm *sorry* you don't love each other any more. It is nearly time for Douglas to start, my dear; go and ask him to come to me.

CONS. Yes—I—I'll—(*going* L.)—I'll tell him you are here. (*Exit* L. 1 E., *still crying.*)

SCOTT. (*Looking after her, with a smile.*) It's a pity they don't love each other any more. I shall make it my personal and professional duty to bring these two wrong-headed young people together—in spite of themselves. Providence, so to speak, has appointed me their attorney. I—*take*—the—case. The devil is the opposing counsel. He's a good lawyer; and highly respected by his fellow-members of the profession. He and I have frequently been on the same side of a case :—I know his tricks. (*Sitting* R.) I dare say a little lying will be necessary. If it is I'll beat him at his own game. Even a lawyer must lie, now and then.

Enter DOUGLAS L. 1 E. *He is in travelling suit.*

DOUG. My dear Scott! (*Taking* SCOTT'S *hand.*)

SCOTT. Douglas!

DOUG. I must apologize for asking you to come here; but I found it impossible, yesterday at the office, to say what I wanted. (*He strikes bell on table,* R. C.) I—I could not say it until the very last moment. (*Enter* MAID *up* R.) Is the carriage at the door, Jeanette?

MAID. Yes, sir.

DOUG. Tell Henry my trunk and valise are ready, and say to my mother and Miss Edith that I will be down in a few moments.

MAID. Yes, sir. (*Exit up* R.)

DOUG. (*Turning to* SCOTT.) I arranged yesterday for you to take the entire management of my property, during my absence.

SCOTT. Yes.

DOUG. I—I also hinted that I should ask you to make certain settlements of my estate. (*A pause.*) My departure for Europe, to-day, is the beginning of a final and absolute—separation—between my—wife—and me.

SCOTT. A—final—separation! The *cause* of this, DOUGLAS?

DOUG. What makes a solid rock fall to pieces without any

apparent cause? The silent and invisible power of a winter's
frost. A frost like that has come upon Constance and
me. (*A slight pause.*) It was my own fault. I gave myself
up to the struggle for wealth. My wife lived alone and neglected, as many another rich man's wife lives—surrounded by
everything a husband's *money* can furnish to make her happy.
One night—not many weeks ago—my mother told me how
cruelly I had neglected Constance—how I had robbed her of a
home. I confessed my wrong to my wife at once. I spoke to
her lovingly. She was silent. At that very moment, the Angel
of Death passed upward with the soul of our little one in his
arms. My child—and my wife's love—were both—dead; it
seemed as if we buried them in the same grave. Since that
night, Constance has been—respectful—and kind to me—but
cold and distant—never the loving wife. We have both lived
within ourselves—strangers to each other in our own home—
husband and wife only to the world. We are nothing to each
other now but—ice.

SCOTT. M—m. (*Glancing at him, then rather carelessly.*) I
hope you'll have a pleasant voyage, Douglas—and a happy
time, on the other side.

DOUG. Happy? Can *you* say " happy "? You?—who knew
us both when we were happy, indeed! How can you mock me
like that? You are cruel, Scott—you are cruel! (*Dropping
his face into his hands,* SCOTT *approaches him,* C. *and extends
his hand.*)

SCOTT. Douglas—(*taking one of his hands in his own*)—I
see you are quite right. You are both of you nothing—but—
ice. (*Looking into* DOUGLAS' *face with a keen glance, still holding his hand;* DOUGLAS *returns his glance, then turns away,* L.
SCOTT *continues, aside, turning* R.) Mount Hecla is nothing
but ice—on the outside. But it's a tolerably lively volcano, for
all that; there's plenty of heat inside.

DOUG. I wish you to—to draw up the papers for an equal
division of my property, between my wife and me—and such
other papers as our—legal—separation—may involve.

SCOTT. No, Douglas!—I cannot. I love you both too
much.

DOUG. I should not have asked you. We must call upon
a stranger, after all. (*Sitting* L. C.)

SCOTT. No!—not to a stranger. If—if it must be done,
you may leave it in my hands. How long will you be away?

DOUG. I cannot tell; years, perhaps. I feel now as if I
could *never* return to America.

SCOTT. You must.

DOUG. Must?

SCOTT. (*Aside.*) Now for my first lie in the case. (*Aloud.*)
I cannot possibly make a division of your property, unless you
are in this country.

DOUG. You have my power of attorney.

SCOTT. In such a case as this, a power of attorney would be

utterly useless. (*Aside.*) He doesn't know anything about law. If another lawyer overheard my legal advice, he'd think *I* didn't. (*Aloud.*) Can't you come back—in three months?

Doug. Three months? Impossible!

Scott. I shall be obliged to leave New York in four months, for the Sandwich Islands—an important case for the United States Government. I may be gone two years. (*Aside.*) The opposite counsel himself can't beat that.

Doug. I cannot confide this matter to any one but you.

Scott. Well then—you must return—in three months.

Doug. (*After a pause.*) Well, I will.

Scott. (*Aside.*) I've gained the first point in the case. The sooner I can bring them together, the harder it'll be for the devil to keep them apart. (*Aloud.*) Constance, of course, understands my relations to—

Doug. We have never spoken on the subject of our final separation.

Scott. Ah!

Doug. Of course, we both understand the situation. But we bade each other good by, a moment ago, without a word.

Scott. You have said good by, already?

Doug. Yes. (*Rising and going up.*) I am simply flying from a life which I can endure no longer. We can write to each other on the subject. We cannot trust our tongues. You, of course, can communicate with Constance, as my representative.

Scott. My dear Douglas—you do not understand the law.

Doug. The law? No.

Scott. (*Aside.*) I don't intend he shall. (*Aloud.*) It is a legal impossibility for me to act in any capacity whatever, between you and your wife, unless you meet her again, personally—at once—and come to an exact mutual understanding as to your respective intentions. De Vinculo Matrimonii—Chapter thirty-seven—section two hundred and thirty-nine—Revised Statutes—1878. (*Aside.*) Lie number three. (*Striking bell on table and rising.*) If I leave them alone together, it's twenty to one he won't go to Europe at all. (*Crosses* L. C.) (*Enter* MAID R.) Please ask Mrs. Winthrop if she will kindly come here. (*Exit* MAID L. 1 E.) Good by, Douglas.

Doug. You will remain?

Scott. I have an immediate engagement. (*Taking out watch.*) It is now after eleven o'clock. I have a case before the Superior Court at eleven-thirty. (*Aside.*) If I keep on lying at this remarkable rate, and with such perfect ease, I'll begin to suspect I'm the devil himself. (*Offers* DOUGLAS *his hand.*)

Doug. Good by, old friend!

Scott. Good by. (*Turning up* C. DOUGLAS *turns to table* R. C.) If the good angels ever do help a lawyer—when he happens to be on their side—I'll win my case.

(*Exit up* R. DOUGLAS *has taken a miniature from the table*, R. C. *He raises it to his lips and is looking at it as* CONSTANCE *enters*, L. 1. E.)

Cons. Douglas.

Doug. Ah—Constance. (*Leaves miniature on the table.*) I have just had an interview with Mr. Scott. I desired to leave a—a very important matter—affecting us both—in his hands. But he has just assured me that he cannot possibly act as our legal adviser in any way whatever unless we come to a—a full mutual understanding as to—as to—the—the relation which we—which we intend to—to bear to each other—hereafter.

Cons. A—a mutual understanding—yes.

Doug. We may be perfectly frank with each other now. We will speak at last what we have both understood for many weeks in our hearts. My departure is only a cloak, of course, to hide the truth for a little time from our friends, and from the world. We—we are about to—to separate—forever.

Cons. Separate—forever !—(*with emotion, almost staggering*) —yes.

Doug. I find it necessary to return in three months. We can then make such—final—and permanent—arrangements—concerning our—our merely legal relations—as we may mutually agree upon. I—I take it for granted that you, no more than I, desire any form of—divorce.

Cons. No—not that.

Doug. We can both trust Mr. Buxton Scott.

Cons. Yes !

Doug. He can draw up a mutual agreement of—separation—in the usual legal form. We *must* meet—once more—to sign it—and—and—that will be the—end.

Cons. The—end—yes. (*Sinks in chair L. C.*)

Doug. While I am away you will remain in this house; and I shall have it transferred to you in the final division of the property. It has many sad memories for both of us ; but we have passed some very happy hours in it, too. The voice of our child, now silent, has made its walls sacred. The ashes of our own love have become cold upon the hearthstone ; but *her* little spirit may still hover about our former home ; and it seems right that it should always find her mother here. Good by, Constance. (*Moving to her and extending his hand.*)

Cons. (*Rising, turning toward him, and placing her hand in his, looking down.*) Good by, Douglas. (*He holds her hand a moment ; then turns up stage. He stops and moves down to the table R. C., taking the child's picture.*)

Doug. Constance, you have other pictures of Rosie. I, too, have another with me. But this one has a value in my eyes that no one else, not even you, could understand. May I take it with me ?

Cons. Yes. Her memory will belong to both of us forever.

Doug. (*Aside.*) I see her face in this—mother and child in one. (*He then moves up R. She looks after him, making a sud-*

*den movement as if to go to him, which she checks. He passes
out rapidly without looking back.*)

OONS. Child and husband—both gone !

CURTAIN.

ACT FOURTH.

SCENE—*Same as that of Act First ; without the child's toys,
and with some changes in the arrangement of the furniture. Small table a little left of C., front, with inkstand and
pens. The portrait of Rosie is absent. No fire. It is now
spring. Afternoon. Edith and Herbert discovered. She
is sitting near her C., sewing. He sits near her, L. C., with a book
in his hand, in a thoughtful attitude, as if he had stopped
reading, losing himself in revery.*

EDITH. It's a very pretty story. Go on, Herbert. I like
to hear you read. You've been silent for a long time.

HER. I've been thinking.

EDITH. What about ?

HER. About *you.*

EDITH. I must go to my room. I haven't given the canary
his bath to-day, and I must see how the old cat and the new
kittens are getting on. (*Rising.*)

HER. No ; please don't go. (*She resumes her seat.*) Edith,
you are so different from what you used to be. You always
run away from me, now—except when some one is with us, or
when I am reading to you,—and whenever I try to tell you
what is in my heart, you change the subject.

EDITH. I must thread my needle again.

HER. (*After a glance and a pause.*) I'll thread it for you.

EDITH. You ! (*Laughing, as she takes thread from spool.*)
I haven't time to wait.

HER. Oh, I *can* thread it. Every young bachelor learns how
to do that. I often have to sew on buttons and things.

EDITH. Well, you may do it.

HER. (*Taking needle and thread.*) Whew !

EDITH. What's the matter ?

HER. It's sharp.

EDITH. (*Laughing.*) Didn't you know that before ? I knew
you'd get into trouble. Mind you thread the right end.

HER. You *like* the story I am reading ?

EDITH. Yes. The part I like best is where love is gradually growing in her heart—without her knowing why—or
where it came from—or what it is.

HER. I can't see anything of that kind in the story.

EDITH. You *can't !*

HER.   She doesn't seem to love him at all, yet.

EDITH.   Oh, yes, she does !

HER.   She always avoids him ; and whenever he tries to make love to her, she finds an excuse for leaving him—or talks about something else.

EDITH.   Why, that's the very sign she loves him.

HER.   Is it, Edith ?   (*Eagerly.*)

EDITH.   Of course !—don't you understand that ?   I'm *sure* she loves him.   I *feel* it, as you go along in the book.

HER.   (*Significantly—looking at her earnestly.*)   That's just the way *you* act to *me.*

EDITH.   Is the needle threaded ?

HER.   One moment.   (*Suddenly beginning to thrust the thread at the eye of the needle.*)

EDITH.   How are you getting on ?

HER.   Splendidly !   We're having a regular set-to.   This is such a *little* fellow !

EDITH.   Ha-ha-ha-ha.

HER.   I can always get ahead of a big one.

EDITH.   Ha-ha-ha.   Hadn't *I* better do it, Herbert ?

HER.   No.   I can do it.   (*With a vigorous thrust.*)

EDITH.   (*After a pause.*)   Isn't the hero of the story funny, Herbert ?

HER.   Funny ?—how ?

EDITH.   He was so frank and bold at first.   But now that she really loves him, he never seems to know what to do or say.

HER.   Oh, *I* understand *him* well enough.

EDITH.   He seems almost afraid of her.

HER.   Of course he does.   That's the way with any man, when he really loves a woman.   (*Looking at her earnestly.*)   *I'm* almost afraid of *you.*

EDITH.   Is the needle ready ?

HER.   I'll hit it in the eye in a moment.   (*Beginning to thrust at the needle again.   He goes on, keeping his eye intently on the needle, and trying to thread it with a variety of motions, ranging from quiet efforts to desperate thrusts.*)   Of course a man can't talk to a woman he loves—(*needle*)—as easily as he can—(*needle*)—to a woman he doesn't love.

EDITH.   In the last chapter you read they were alone together nearly an hour, and he never said a word about love.

HER.   He was coming to the subject half a dozen times—(*needle*)—and she always turned him off.

EDITH.   But she was *thinking* about it.

HER.   How could he tell that ?

EDITH.   He might have guessed it.

HER.   I don't see how he could guess that she was *thinking* about love (*paying great attention to needle*)—when she was *talking* about her old cat and new kittens—(*needle*)—or her canary's bath.

EDITH.   I don't remember that in the book.

HER.   Eh !—Oh !—No.

EDITH. There's nothing about a cat or a canary in the story you were reading.

HER. *You* know the story I am thinking about. (*Rising and leaning over her, speaking earnestly.*) Do you remember, Edith, one night last winter, I told you I hoped to have a little home of my own?

EDITH. Yes. (*Dropping her head.*)

HER. And I said, I—I hoped to get—married.

EDITH. Yes.

HER. You didn't know what I meant—when I told you—I loved you.

EDITH. I—I never dreamed of such a thing as love till that night.

HER. I tried to teach you what it was.

EDITH. It seems as if I had lived years since then. (*Rising, and turning* R.)

HER. (*With deep earnestness.*) Edith—I love you—with all my soul!—but I feel as if *I* could learn from *you* now. I hardly dare ask for your love. It could not be stronger than mine—but it would be better and sweeter and purer.

EDITH. (*After a slight pause.*) You need not ask for it. It belongs to you.

HER. My darling! (*Embracing her.*) I shall be your guide and your protector through life!

EDITH. O Herbert—I am so happy! (*Her head resting on his breast.*)

HER. Whew!

EDITH. (*Starting up.*) What is it, Herbert?

HER. That needle.

EDITH. (*Sympathetically.*) O—h;—where is it? (*Taking his hand, which he puts in hers, and touching different parts with her finger.*) Here?

HER. No.

EDITH. Here?

HER. No.

EDITH. Here?

HER. Yes—there.

EDITH. A—h! (*Putting his hand to her lips.*)

HER. We can look after the old cat and the new kittens, now.

Exeunt R. 1 E. *Enter* CONSTANCE *up* R. *She moves down* R. C., *glancing at clock on mantel.*

CONS. Will the time never come? Oh! I wish to-day were past.

Enter MRS. RUTH *up* L., *in bonnet, etc.*

MRS. RUTH. Constance!—I have just left Douglas—at his hotel. He has told me the worst! This afternoon you are to sign the papers that separate you forever.

CONS. Yes. *I could* not tell you.

MRS. RUTH. When Douglas did not come to his own home,

I knew, for the first time, how wide the gulf between you had become. Isit too late?

CONS. Yes!—too late. (*Crossing* R.)

MRS. RUTH. Douglas said the same. (*Passing* CONSTANCE, *and moving toward the door* R. 1 E.) My heart is full. (*She stops near door with her hands over her face ; rouses herself and turns.*) I—I shall always love you, Constance, as my own child!

CONS. Mother! (*Going to her.*)

MRS. RUTH. (*Embracing her.*) My daughter! (*She kisses her and goes out* R. 1 E. CONSTANCE *stands looking after her.*)

Enter MAID *up* L., *with a card.*

CONS. I can see no one to-day, Jeanette—(*Takes card*)—except—Mr. Buxton Scott will be here—you may admit him at once. (*Exit* MAID *up* L. CONSTANCE *reads card.*) " Mrs.—Richard—Chetwyn."

MRS. DICK. (*Putting her head in at door, up* L.) How d' y' do?

CONS. Barbara?

MRS. DICK. Dick and I have got married again. I'm using the same old cards. May I come in?

CONS. Certainly.

MRS. DICK. I'll tell you all about it. (*Sitting beside her.*) It was private. We found that being divorced was worse than being incompatible. We were both awfully lonely. Ha-ha-ha! Dick and I went through our courtship all over again, just as if we'd never been married at all. Poor Aunt Jane had another dreadful time with me.

CONS. What do you mean?

MRS. DICK. Aunt Jane Vandeveer brought me up, you know. The dear old maid! I've always been her favorite niece. She's going to leave me all her money. I went to stay with Aunt Jane again after Dick and I were separated. She was more particular with me than she was when I was a young lady. Ha-ha-ha! One day Aunt Jane and I passed Dick on Madison Avenue. Of course we didn't bow to each other. But Dick winked at me. Aunt Jane saw it. She was fearfully indignant. The next time we met—Aunt Jane was on the opposite side of me—*I* winked at *Bob*—I mean *Dick*. After that we carried on a regular flirtation with each other. He used to pass the house and wave his handkerchief. Aunt Jane always closed the parlor shutters with a bang, and I kissed my hand to him out of the second story window. Ha-ha-ha! Then Dick sent me a secret note by one of the servants. We arranged a clandestine meeting in Stuyvesant Square ; and we went down to Long Beach together. Dick said sweet things to me all the afternoon, just as he did when we first fell in love ; and after it was dark, we wandered off on the beach by ourselves, in the moonlight—and I had tears in my eyes—and

Dick kissed me—and the next day we ran away and got married.

CONS. You—you ran away—with your own husband?

MRS. DICK. I *had* to. Aunt Jane says she'll never forgive us. But she *will*. I always did run away to get married. Dick and I are having another honeymoon.

CONS. I—I am very glad you are happy again, Barbara.

MRS. DICK. Thank you, my dear; I knew you would be. I—I wish *you* were happy, too, Constance. (*In a serious tone.*)

CONS. I?

MRS. DICK. Forgive me, Constance—but—I—I know things aren't quite as they should be. Perhaps I know more than I ought to. Women always *do*. Your husband hasn't been here since he landed; and that was two weeks ago. I am so happy now with Dick—I don't like to see you miserable; and I feel as if *I* might have had something to do with it.

CONS. You?

MRS. DICK. I was always such a thoughtless creature! One night last winter I told you how Dick found Douglas at Mrs. Dunbar's house once or twice. I thought it was great fun then; but I shouldn't think so now. When I was a grass widow I often met Mrs. Dunbar. She's a grass widow, too, you know. Grass widows always do meet each other; and they always talk about the infelicities of married life. That's one reason I'm glad to join the army of married women again. Mrs. Dunbar told me that it was nothing but a *business* connection with Mr. Winthrop and her.

Enter MAID *up* L.

MAID. Mr. Scott is here, madam.

MRS. DICK. He's the very man.

CONS. Ask him to come in here, Jeanette. (*Exit* MAID.) What do you mean, Barbara?

MRS. DICK. Mrs. Dunbar said Buxton Scott knew all about it. Ask *him*, my dear, at once. I'll leave you with him. Is your mother in?

CONS. Yes.

MRS. DICK. I'll run and tell her about Dick and me. I know she'll be glad to hear it.   (*Exit* R. 1 E.

Enter BUXTON SCOTT, *up* L.)

SCOTT. Constance, my dear! I am very sorry to come on such an errand. (*Taking her hand.*) Is there anything you wish to say to me before Douglas arrives?

CONS. Yes; I wish to ask you a question. Have you ever had any business connection with—Mr. Winthrop—and—and Mrs. Hepworth Dunbar?

SCOTT. Mrs. — Dunbar? (*Aside.*) Of course!—I might have known a woman would pop up somewhere in this case. (*Aloud.*) Yes, Constance, I had. But that is a professional confidence.

CONS. As you please, Mr. Scott. It is not a matter that can now affect the future relations of Mr. Winthrop and me. We can never come together again. But it is not too late for me to—be—*just*—if I have wronged him.

SCOTT. (*Aside.*) I'll be hanged if I give the devil a single point in the case—even for the sake of my professional honor; *he* doesn't care a rap for *his* professional honor. (*Aloud.*) I'll tell you the whole truth, Constance. Your brother Clarence—

CONS. Clarence! what of him?

SCOTT. He was a confidential clerk, and he speculated in stocks—like many another young man. Result—a defalcation —fifty thousand dollars.

CONS. Defalcation!

SCOTT. Douglas *saved* him from imprisonment and disgrace —(*she starts*)—by meeting the whole amount himself, out of his own fortune.

CONS. Imprisonment—disgrace! (*Sinking in chair* R. C.)

SCOTT. It was impossible to prevent the *criminal arrest* of Clarence without the consent of *all* the creditors. The only one that refused was Mrs. Hepworth Dunbar, to whom a large amount of the misplaced securities belonged. She had certain social grudges to make good; Mr. Douglas Winthrop had declined to allow his wife to be introduced to Mrs. Dunbar. She had now an opportunity to disgrace the family. Your husband was compelled to call upon her—frequently—in person. His last call was late one night. Clarence would have been arrested the next day. Douglas's appeal was in vain. He was called suddenly from her house that night by a messenger from home. On the following morning I called on Mrs. Dunbar myself. I told her that the child of Douglas Winthrop had died the night before. Even a woman like that has a heart. Mrs. Dunbar had lost a child herself; and the memory of her own sorrow made her merciful. Your brother was saved. His—fault—is a secret .(*Enter* DOUGLAS, *up* L. SCOTT *turns.*) Douglas.

> (*Nodding and moving up* C. DOUGLAS *bows to him.* CONSTANCE *turns, and they look at each other a moment ; then* DOUGLAS *moves across and down to her* R., *extending his hand frankly, and taking her hand.*

DOUG. Constance. (*He holds her hand a moment ; then drops it ; both standing a moment in silence, looking down.*

CONS. Douglas—I—I have this moment heard of a great kindness you have done my brother and—me. (DOUGLAS *glances sharply up at* SCOTT.) Do not blame *him*. I *asked* him to tell me. I—(*with deep feeling*)—I thank you, Douglas.

DOUG. I only did what *any* man of proper feeling would have done under the same circumstances. (*A long silence, both looking down.*)

DOUG. (*Crossing* L.) Mr. Scott, we will proceed with the business before us. (SCOTT *up* C., *looks from one to the other,*

alternately, several times ; then moves down to table, near c.,
front.)

SCOTT. I have drawn up four documents. (*Taking papers
from his pocket.*) These two are duplicates. (*Reads endorse-
ment on one of the papers.*) " Douglas Winthrop and Constance Winthrop—Deed of Separation."

> (DOUGLAS *and* CONSTANCE *sit* L. *and* R., SCOTT *sits at
> table ; opens the paper ; and reads in a rapid, business-
> like tone.*)

"This indenture, made the seventh day of May, eighteen hundred and eighty-two, by and between Douglas Winthrop, of the
city and State of New York, party of the first part, and Constance Winthrop, of the same place, party of the second part—
Witnesseth : Whereas the said parties of the first and second
parts were lawfully united in wedlock on the twenty-eighth day
of June, in the year"— (*He stops suddenly in his quick reading ;
the tone of his voice changing, and speaking slowly, with natural
feeling.*) I remember that day perfectly. We all drove to the
church together from the old homestead, near Concord. The
marriage service never seemed so beautiful to me as it did
that morning. Your dear old father's voice, Constance, had
more than a pastor's tenderness in it as he uttered the words
which you both repeated after him—" for better, for worse, in
sickness and in health, to love and to cherish, until death us
do part." (CONSTANCE *and* DOUGLAS *rise to their feet* R. *and*
L., *showing signs of rising emotion, as* SCOTT *proceeds.*) When
you knelt at the chancel-rail before him, his voice was trembling
as he repeated that beautiful prayer : Send thy blessing upon
these thy servants ; that they may ever remain in perfect love
and peace together. (CONSTANCE *and* DOUGLAS *drop their
heads sadly.*) As he pronounced the blessing—of a pastor and
father in one—the sun came from behind a cloud—and the
light streamed through the window on your heads. Douglas'
mother was leaning on my arm. (CONSTANCE *and* DOUGLAS
turn up stage R. *and* L., *standing with backs to audience and
their heads bowed deeply.*) There were tears in her eyes, but a
smile shone through them ; as if the love of a mother's heart
was pouring *its* blessing upon both her children—like the sunshine through the window. (*His voice is a little broken, and
he brushes a tear from his eye with his handkerchief.*) But
(*brushes away another tear, leaving handkerchief on table*)—hem—
this is a digression. We will proceed with the business
before us.

—DOUG. (*With choking voice.*) Please read the papers as
rapidly as possible, Mr. Scott.

CONS. We—(*choking*)—we need not delay more than is—
absolutely—necessary.

SCOTT. (*Resuming his rapid business tone ; reading.*) " And
whereas said parties of the first and second parts"—but we
shall not sign this instrument until we have considered the

other papers. We will dispose of them at once. (*Putting down
the Deed of Separation, taking up another paper and rising.*)
This is a deed whereby Douglas Winthrop conveys in fee simple
to Constance Winthrop the old homestead where she was born,
near Concord, Massachusetts. (*Pause.*) Some of the happiest
hours of my life were passed there. You two children were
always running about the place. Constance was a perfect
little tom-boy. Ha-ha-ha! You both gave me a particularly
warm reception, one day, when I had just arrived from New
York. I was going up the gravel walk. Your father was
coming down the steps to meet me. Constance came bounding
around the corner, and you after her. She was *running* one
way and *looking* the other. As your father was helping me to
my feet, he remarked that those children were *always* upset-
ting something. Ha-ha! Five minutes after that, Douglas
was in the cherry-tree, and you were holding up your little
apron for the fruit;—the old cherry-tree down in the corner,
near the summer-house.

CONS. Oh, *no*—the cherry-tree was in the *other* corner.

DOUG. Over near the old well.

SCOTT. So it was. When you both grew older, I often saw
you walking arm in arm, on the lawn—after the stars came
out. Constance was always explaining to me that you were
giving her lessons in—astronomy. You were quite as likely
to be telling her where the stars were, in the afternoon,
as at night. Those were delightful days at the old homestead.

DOUGLAS and CONSTANCE. Delightful! (*With thoughtful
manner, as if the force of old memories was beginning to
influence them.*)

SCOTT. You had a lover's quarrel about that time. Constance had given you a pair of slippers she had been working
for you. When you quarrelled she took them away from you,
and gave them to *me*. I remember, Constance had a little
dark bay pony.

CONS. Oh, no!—(*moving to R. C., near SCOTT*)—it was gray.

DOUG. With a black spot on the left shoulder. (*Moving
down L. C.*)

SCOTT. Dappled gray—so it was. His name was Jack.

CONS. Oh, no !

DOUG. No !

CONS. It was Jenny.

SCOTT. Oh, yes—of course—Jenny. The first time Douglas
helped you to mount—Jenny—(*turning to DOUGLAS*)—you
gave her too strong a lift !

DOUG. Yes. (*With a smile.*)

SCOTT. (*To CONSTANCE.*) You fell over on the other side !

CONS. Yes. (CONSTANCE *and* DOUGLAS *laugh gently and
pleasantly.* SCOTT *laughs with them quietly, moving back a step.*)

SCOTT. The old family carriage horse—*his* name was Jack.

DOUG. *He* was dark bay. (*To CONSTANCE.*) You used to

drive Jack for your father—(*stepping to her in front of* SCOTT) —when he made his pastoral visits. (SCOTT *gradually retires up stage* L.)

CONS. I always sat in the carriage, to keep the flies off Jack.

DOUG. I often met you on the road; and I used to think you were doing as pious a work outside, making the old horse comfortable, as your father was doing inside.

CONS. Old Jack was one of the family. Dear old Jack!

DOUG. Dear old Jack!

SCOTT. (*Up* L. C.) Dear old Jack! (*He stands up* L., *pretending to look over deed, but watching them.*)

DOUG. Do you remember *one* such afternoon, Constance?— You were sitting in front of the little house where the old sexton's widow lived.

CONS. (*Smiling.*) How often we used to run down there when we were children! (*Sitting front.*)

DOUG. Yes—she always had fresh doughnuts for us, on Saturdays. (*Sitting at her side near the table.* CONSTANCE *nods, smiling.*) But we had grown older, at the time I am thinking of now. I joined you in the carriage. I—I asked you a question, that afternoon. (*Taking her hand.*) Do you remember your answer?

CONS. Yes. (*As if lost in memory.*)

DOUG. That was the very word! I asked you to be—my wife. Oh, Constance!—I was the happiest man in the world.

SCOTT. They're doing very well *without* a lawyer. (*Exit up* L.)

DOUG. We were in the shade of the great elm. Old Jack turned his head and looked back at us, as if he was giving us his consent. This ring—(*referring to one on her finger*)— was the pledge of the promises we made to each other, that day. Our initials are engraved inside of it.

CONS.—And the word—"Forever."

DOUG. When I placed it on your finger, in the dear old home—(*gradually extending his arm about her waist*)—I drew you to me—(*raising her hand toward his lips*)—and I— (*He suddenly stops; his eye resting upon the Deed of Separation, on the table near him. He slowly withdraws his arm and drops her hand; reaches forward and takes the paper; finally holding it in both hands before him and looking at it steadily.* CONSTANCE *looks at the paper, draws up, rises, and walks* R. DOUGLAS *starts to his feet, drops the paper upon the table, and turns up* L., *under strong emotion. He stands for a moment, before speaking, as if collecting his thoughts and bringing his feelings under control.*) We—we were losing ourselves—in—in *dreams* of the past.

CONS. We had forgotten the—the *present.*

DOUG. (*As if suddenly seeing* SCOTT *out* L., *and beckoning with a nervous movement.*) Ah—Mr. Scott—Mr. Scott! (*He walks down* L., *a few steps. Re-enter* SCOTT, *up* L. *The deed, folded, is still in his hand. He stops* C., *and looks* R. *and* L.)

SCOTT. I beg your pardon. I left my handkerchief in my hat outside. (*Moving down* C. *He discovers his handkerchief on the table ; picks it up quickly, and thrusts it into his pocket, g'ancing each way. He then begins to read very rapidly from the deed in his hand.*) "Said party of the first part does by these presents grant, sell, remise, release, convey and confirm— m—m—m—heirs and assigns forever the premises hereinafter described—m—m—m—m—namely, to wit—South side of the Boston High-road—intersection of the county line—thence in a southerly direction along the western bank of the Coolsac Creek"— Speaking of the Coolsac Creek, by the by—(*dropping suddenly to a conversational tone*)—I saw the same old clump of willows on the opposite bank, when I was there last summer. That was a sort of meeting-place for young lovers. I remember, one day—I met Douglas and a lady there. You remember it, Douglas—what *was* her name ? It was Douglas and Miss—(*turning to* CONSTANCE, *who draws up sharply and looks around.* DOUGLAS *looks in surprise*)—that particular friend of yours, Constance—Miss—Kate—Miss—really, I—

CONS. Kate Fairfield !

SCOTT. Yes—that's the name. Douglas was arranging a bunch of violets in her hair. But this is a digression. I beg your pardon. (*Reads rapidly.*) "With all and singular the tenements, hereditaments, and appurtenances thereunto belonging ; and the said party of the first part"—

DOUG. Pardon me, Mr. Scott—but you are mistaken ;— I was never at the place you refer to with Miss Kate Fairfield.

CONS. (*With great dignity and signs of rising jealousy.*) Mr. Scott's memory may be more accurate than yours.

DOUG. But I protest—I—

CONS. You were saying, Mr. Scott ?—

SCOTT. Let me see—it was—no—ah—now I think again— I got you young people so mixed up when I recall those days— it was Mr. Lawrence Armytage—and—Constance. (DOUGLAS *and* CONSTANCE *both start.*)

CONS. Nothing of the kind ! (*Moving down,* R., *a few steps, indignantly.* SCOTT *turns up stage,* C., *standing with his back to the audience, and looking up at a picture on the wall.*)

DOUG. Mr. Lawrence Armytage was *frequently* at the house —when *I* called.

CONS. Kate Fairfield lived on the highroad between your house and mine.

DOUG. Mr. Armytage had always dropped in—to see—your *father.*

CONS. Whenever you were late — you — (*choking*) — you always said it was the old sexton's widow ! (*Angrily, crossing to him* L.) I saw you, myself—talking with Kate Fairfield, over the gate—while I was passing in the carriage with father —the very day before I took away your slippers and gave them to Mr. Scott—and I'm *glad* I *did* it ! (*Drawing up before him angrily; then turning her back on him; and returning* R., *with a dignity in absurd contrast with the words and situation.*)

DOUG. (*Following her* R.) And the very day after that you discovered that I was only asking Miss Fairfield if *her* mother would lend *my* mother the hemmer of her sewing-machine!—and you took the slippers away from Mr. Scott and sent them back to *me!*

CONS. Oh! (*He returns* L., *triumphantly. She turns toward him.*) I *didn't* send them back to you!

DOUG. You?—(*Turning suddenly.*)—Mr. Scott! (*Appealing earnestly to* SCOTT, *up stage.*)

SCOTT. Eh? (*Jumping around suddenly.*)

CONS. (*To* SCOTT.) He says *I* sent those slippers back to him. You *know* I didn't—don't you?

SCOTT. Certainly, you didn't. (*Starting down* C.)

DOUG. The package was addressed in *her* handwriting.

SCOTT. Yes—Constance wrote the address. (*Still moving down.*)

CONS. Mr. Scott *sent* it—by the boy—himself.

SCOTT. Yes—I *sent* it. (C., *front.*)

DOUG. It is quite immaterial;—I dare say you sent another pair to Mr. Armytage!

CONS. O—o—o—o—o—h! (*Bursting into sobs,* R. C. DOUGLAS *stands* L. C., *with his arms folded.* SCOTT *looks from one to the other a moment.*

SCOTT. Ah, by the way, it has just occurred to me: it was Mr. Armytage and Miss Fairfield I saw together under the willows.

CONS. Oh. (*Looking up from her sobs.*) It wasn't *either* of us.

SCOTT. When I saw Douglas in the lane—*you* were with him, Constance.

DOUG. Oh. It was *both* of us.

SCOTT. (*To* DOUGLAS.) You had been gathering some water-lilies for Constance.

CONS. Oh, yes! (*Brightly, with sudden recollection.*)

SCOTT. (*To* CONSTANCE.) It was the day he fell into the pond.

DOUG. Yes!

SCOTT. He got into the mud up to the knees.

CONS. I remember!

DOUG. So do I!

SCOTT. (*To* DOUGLAS.) Constance tried to pull you out of the water; and (*To* CONSTANCE) he pulled you *in!* (CONSTANCE *and* DOUGLAS *burst into a merry laugh, nodding at each other across* SCOTT.) We will proceed with the business before us. (*Their faces suddenly drop. They turn up stage* R. *and* L.) Returning to the original Deed of Separation. (*Taking up the Deed.* CONSTANCE *and* DOUGLAS *look up at each other, across stage, at back; then drop their eyes.* SCOTT *reads.*) "The said Douglas Winthrop and the said Constance Winthrop, his wife, have by mutual consent agreed to live separate and apart from each other;—and whereas the aforesaid"— (*Enter* EDITH R. 1 E.) Edith !

EDITH. Mr. Scott !

SCOTT. (*Going to her.*) I have some news for you, Edith. Your brother Douglas is here.

EDITH. Oh!—where is he ?

(*He leads her to* DOUGLAS, *who meets her* L. C.)

EDITH. Douglas ! (*Throwing her arms about his neck.*)

DOUG. Edith—my little sister !

EDITH. Oh—I am so *glad* you have come home—so glad ! We shall all be happy, now.

DOUG. Happy !—Yes.

EDITH. Constance has missed you so much, Douglas—so much ! You won't go away from us again—will you ?

DOUG. I—I—

SCOTT. My little pet ! (*Taking her from* DOUGLAS, *who turns up stage a few steps.*)

EDITH. H'm!

SCOTT. I know you have a great deal to tell, Douglas, but not now. ' Sit down, Edith. (*Leading her to seat* L.)

EDITH. Oh, very well—I will wait. But I *am* so glad Douglas is home again.

DOUG. (*Apart—in* SCOTT'S *ear.*) We—we *cannot* go on with this—in *her* presence.

SCOTT. (*Apart to him.*) I need not read the rest of the paper. You and Constance can sign it—in silence. (DOUGLAS *retires from him and turns up* C., *a little to the right, dropping his head.* CONSTANCE *stands* R., *partly up stage.* SCOTT *returns to the table, near* C., *front ; takes up the Deed of Separation and turns, facing* CONSTANCE *and* DOUGLAS.) There is one piece of property not mentioned in any of these deeds;—a burial lot in Greenwood Cemetery, with one little grave. (*A pause,* CONSTANCE *and* DOUGLAS *looking down, with bowed heads.*)

EDITH. Mother and I went to Greenwood yesterday, Douglas. You and Constance must go with us next time. The place where Rosie lies is covered with flowers. (CONSTANCE *and* DOUGLAS *give way to their tears, both dropping their faces into their hands.*)

SCOTT. Even a lawyer cannot divide that property, nor the memories of a father and mother that cluster about the grave of their child :—and there is a little soul that belongs to you both. (*He turns to the table, turning over the leaves of the Deed to the last page.*) You—you will both sign—here—if you please. (*He takes up the pen, dips it into the ink, and turns, holding it toward them. During this action they have rushed into each other's arms, weeping. Picture.* SCOTT *turns and drops the pen, taking the deed and tearing it.*) I have won the case. (*He walks up* C. *Enter* MRS. RUTH R. 1. E. *She starts, with an exclamation, looking at* DOUGLAS *and* CONSTANCE, *with her back to the audience.* DOUGLAS *looks up to her and meets her down* R., *embracing her.*

Enter HERBERT, *up* L. *Places a ring upon* EDITH'S *first finger. Enter* MRS. DICK R. 1. E., *sailing in rapidly.*

MRS. DICK. (*As she enters.*) I've been away from Dick ·for nearly two hours. (*She turns* C., *seeing* DOUGLAS.) Mr. Winthrop! (*Goes to him and takes his hand.*)

DOUG. (*smiling.*) Mrs. Dick !

MRS. DICK. Constance ! (*Turning to* CONSTANCE.) I really must go. Dick'll be lonely. We haven't been separated so long since we've been married—this time. Good by, all. (*Going up* L., *nods to* SCOTT *as she passes him up* C.) Ah—Mr. Scott.

SCOTT. Mrs. Mackenzie !

MRS. DICK. (*Stopping up* L. C., *turning.*) Mrs. Chetwyn.

SCOTT. Eh ?

MRS. DICK. Dick and I have got married again.

SCOTT. Married ? You and—allow me. · (*Offers her a card.*) My professional card.

MRS. DICK. Thank you—no. We've had quite enough of the law ; and if we ever go anywhere by way of Connecticut, we'll take through tickets. Call on us, Mr. Scott—any evening —Dick and I are always at home. (*Exit up* L.)

SCOTT. The devil has lost that case, too.

DOUG. (*To* MRS. RUTH, *with one arm about* CONSTANCE'S *waist ; raising her hand in his and looking at the ring on her finger.*) Dear mother, our hearts have conquered us. (*Turning to* CONSTANCE.) We can trust to them hereafter.

CON. (*Looking down at the ring.*) Yes, Douglas, " Forever."

CURTAIN.

I was associated with the original Madison
Square Theatre for a couple of years. It was
a great company. The theatre was the
smallest in New York at the time; with but
a tiny stage. It has been long demolished.
Although have no recollection of playing in
" Young Mrs. Winthrop", yet the marks in
front of the character of Douglas, must
indicate my having played the part. If so,
it was more than likely with one of the
travelling companies.
Charles, and Daniel Frohman, were in those
days the guiding hands of this famous
theatre.

                        Fred Ross.

www.ingramcontent.com/pod-product-compliance
Lightning Source LLC
Chambersburg PA
CBHW032141270626
47172CB00009B/785